Aberrant Literature Short Fiction Collection

Volume III

Edited by

Jason Peters

www.AberrantLiterature.com

@AberrantLit

Hello from Aberrant Literature,

Thanks so much for checking out this collection of some of the most inventive and creative short fiction you're likely to come across. At Aberrant Literature, our goal is for you to have a unique experience via the power of creative fiction. It is our belief that in a literary landscape populated by recycled and tired ideas, there are many unique and wonderful voices looking for an audience, and it is our aim to bring them to you. It is our sincere hope that you will appreciate the level of ingenuity on display, and will join us on our journey as we search the country for the best and most creative short fiction on the horizon.

Stay Aberrant,

Jason Peters

Editor-In-Chief

Table of Contents

The Life and Times of a Private Tick

by Carl Reid

The first thing you've gotta know is they never slink in, sultry and purring like they do in the movies. *The old movies.* Maybe you don't even know what the hell I'm talking about; depends on your era. But either way, that's a timeless truth; that image is fiction.

Typically, a client will call. Sometimes it's an email or a vid, but if they're serious, people are smart enough to know that a call will still get you an immediate response—making it significantly more likely a Tick will take the job. If I'm gonna shoot every one of my particles back fifty years through the Continuum, at the very least, I wanna feel some kind of connection to the person buying me the ticket. Most of all, I want to be certain that they're paying roundtrip. So, yeah, a live voice helps.

But just as important, the biggest advantage of speaking over the phone is ID Rec software that gets the process moving. Won't work on words on a screen, and, again, vids are so infrequent, not much use installing it there, though the reference data would be unquestionably greater. But, voice analysis, syntax matrices, and vocab cross-references amply do the trick. The polygraph is a junk add-on, though; *total* bullshit. A real Tick always goes with his gut.

Once I had her identity verified, I let her continue; someplace public. Always make the first meeting high-profile and in the daylight (only if you prefer your head someplace above your neck, that is, and you don't have any gripes with breathing). It was an unusual case only in the breadth of the crime. Your typical wackadoo, aspiring serial only makes it to two bodies before he gets sloppy and someone, typically the Chron Cops (if they can secure a warrant) busts them and preserves the Line. This guy, somehow, made it to four: three women and one man; unidentified.

She wanted me to figure that out, the final vic's name. I told her what she already knew—that it didn't work like that. If anyone had ever solved it, it would already be in the records. *All of this has already happened.* Didn't mean, though, that I couldn't play a role in catching him...or at the very least, provide her with whatever firsthand details she may have wanted to know. It's not exactly pleasant work, but if a few snapshots of the grizzly aftermath are what it takes for a Grade-A, gen-mod yuppie to achieve some sense of closure (or possibly "climax," if the screeners forgot to remove a few of those bad genes), who am I to judge if the check clears?

Tessa Dunlap Abernathy. Tess. Her parents must have had a not-so-clandestine love affair with late twentieth century strippers. Now, looks-wise, she fit the cinema clichés. But then again, like I said, what nucleotide-altered woman with that kind of money didn't nowadays? Eternally engorged lips; flowing, auburn curls down to the middle of her back that mockingly flicked-off middle-age; a waist you could almost fit one hand around; and emerald green eyes that supernaturally caught the light, whatever part of the room she stood in. She was, of course, in a word, gorgeous, but she was equally mundane.

I'd taken more jobs from Doll People like her than I could possibly remember, and the reason I succeed in this business is because my memory is pretty fucking good. Sadly, Tess here, in all her grafted, ethereal elegance, would be forgotten the moment I took the time to recall my pin number. Perhaps, I wondered, as I avoided being trapped in those endless, emerald whirlpools to admire the titillating grout on the coffee shop floor, I was making it easier on myself that way. A woman like that could never go back in time without uprooting the modern world. But a guy like me...well, I guess I had a face for radio. *I was born for this.*

To my initial surprise, she was nervous. Maybe she hadn't had dealings with my "element" before. Wouldn't be shocked. But she was kind, and smiled - which is rare - each time, unconsciously undoing the masterwork of her face's engineer by slowly adding two, small creases. I couldn't help but focus on them. That, I would remember.

She had the typical story; nothing I hadn't heard before. Divorcee with a ton of time and even more money after the papers were filed. The children were grown, so now was the time to "focus on herself"; get back in touch with who she is. Which, I suppose, means digging through the lives of long-dead people you've never met. Thank the Lord for those genealogy guys; they give me a quarter of my business.

I suppose they zero in on the spiciest stories, which is why the scumbags and murderers always float to the top. And then, I suppose, what guilt already comes from teething on a silver spoon gets exponentially amplified when you learn some fucker in your family's past may have murdered, raped, or pillaged to earn said cutlery. Never looked into it myself, since, you know, guilt and "introspective reflection" aren't really my forte, but at the very least, I can follow the psychology: *The bedrock of my identity is built upon a rotten, infested foundation; what can I do to set things right?* Well, I suppose it makes sense you'd call an exterminator.

The pest's name was Ryan Cooper Hanes, four generations back on her father's side. He didn't earn the clan much of anything, save unwanted notoriety, but he was a black spot on the resume that needed to be removed. For the Doll People, the name was the most prized piece in the vault. And now that she'd gone back to hers again, the rebirth had to be completely pure.

I asked her why she came to me and not the Chrons. They'd sweep this up in a jiffy, at no cost if she had an Artifact to give them. She replied with the one word I hate the most in this biz. *Destiny*. But before I could launch into my diatribe about my inalienable right of choice, causality, and Humanity's inherent free will, she powered up her tab and shut me down. My jaw dropped as I stared myself in the face through the blockade of a crime-scene in 2013. I was time-displaced, watching Ryan Cooper Hanes being handcuffed by Conventionals and hauled away.

I forgot the really salient point I was ready to make about "free will" as I took another thirty seconds to help my brain digest the full-course meal of the image before me. *Touche', Tess. Coffee's on me.*

The next few steps were simple, and since I knew, for a fact now, that I'd be going for the ride, I didn't have to worry about acing the bureaucracy. I filed a Petition for Chronal Displacement under the auspices of "Criminal Investigation" and gave them my license number. No muss and nothing tricky. It'd take the standard eight to ten days as the Chrons ran a Temporal Integrity Check to make sure no one had previously jumped to that particular moment and started fraying Space-Time's precious fabric. Too many tachyons swirling about one particular era and shit gets weird…or so we're told. Wormholes. Singularities. *Bad Shit* in capital letters.

Since I found myself walking out the door with gravity securing my dad's shitty loafers snugly to the ground, and I wasn't, at the moment, being eternally stretched into an infinite string of human spaghetti, it would seem as if no one had fucked up quite that badly yet. So, I went speedily on my way, supremely confident in my inevitable stamp of approval. And, not that I usually do, but I didn't give the matter one more moment's thought. *Thanks to that picture.* And with my mind sunny and free, I could devote the sum of my attention to packing for my trip.

The research was fairly straightforward. I'd been five years out from that era before, in both directions. But it's something of an exact science picking out a wardrobe. Reference photos help. Lord knows enough freelance jumpers have made a quick buck documenting *Humanity Through the Ages* for the evolving scientific database, but with clothes, you have to be careful. Come down in a pair of Jordans circa two years in the relative future (particularly in the city), and you're gonna be noticed. *And it's gonna be a problem.* Arrive in a Von Dutch hat, five years past the trend, and you really stand out—for crooked looks or an ass-kicking. So, rule of thumb is it's best to play it safe, and just buy generic.

For example, you'd have better luck arriving in the early oughts in a full cowboy outfit than a FUBU jacket, because at least people's first instinct would be that you were in costume, and not that you're a man displaced in time. Luckily though, around 2010, the "retro" fashions grow back in style, so anything from the late-seventies to the nineties, provided they can still be made (polyester is a no-go), won't garner too much attention for the ensuing ten years. This is very much a blessing, since skinny jeans, literally and figuratively, never suited me (or my shot putter's ankles), and bellbottoms are, therefore, my close, personal friends. But why try for anything too risky when Levis will have you covered for four decades, and you only need one pair? I make the call and choose to pack light.

All the other gear was a little more heavy-duty than the shit I'd take on a baseline jaunt. Again, I'd bested my share of sickos, but this batter had talent, so I wasn't about to take any chances. Typically, most jumps for most Ticks aren't like this at all. Half the time, you're going back, stalking an old lady for a few weeks to see which ottoman grandma dashed away the inheritance in, or following up on that *other* old lady's hunch that her hubby wasn't at the poker game the night he came home reeking of off-brand Chanel (going generic not really of much help to anyone at that moment). Yeah, that was the usual grind—upper-crust gossip and Junior Paparazzo Academy training: dutifully sorting the patrician refuse. We aren't called "Ticks" just for the shitty time pun. *Blueblood is all we live on.*

But that was all right, 'cause a little blood never fazed me; neither did much else, for that matter. In fact, I could guess the fastest way she ID'd the man in that picture was by asking around which PI would be game for something like this. Smart wager would have my name surface in the top three. Some guys are born assholes, looking for a fight— former Chron-types who miss the action with an unquenchable case of Tachyon Thirst. Others, they just use what they were given to help them make their way, usually *through* someone else. Me? I'm somewhere in between if I don't think too hard about it…and I'm sober. But there's no such thing as bad marketing, in this or any business, so I'll take whatever reputation sticks. So, therefore, if my calling card reads, "Rough and Tumble," I'll do my best to leave the paying customer satisfied.

Implying a hunt like this takes any kind of skill, even across decades, is a PI blowing smoke up your ass or trying to get laid. They don't come to me 'cause I'm trained in Forensics or earned a Masters in Criminal Psychology; that's not how you win this war. I leave that shit to the Chrons, who always get the first shot at patching up The Fabric's worn, loose ends. Like I said, what we do is clean up the mess—and when you're a janitor, all you really need is the right broom. I beat these inbred butchers and kiddie rapists by being, in all ways, an evolved state of Man—with superior firepower. I have tech and a prior knowledge to track, snuff, and tag any Paleolith you'll sic me on, no matter how clever or deranged, because even the smartest Neanderthal is just a Neanderthal. He's using shale and two sticks when I'm bringing a flamethrower. I ran down the list and tested the weight. My bags were ready.

And that was that. I didn't need to waste my time peering into his childhood; finding the root of his malfunction. When he was touched, where he was touched—by Daddy, Mommy, or Weird Uncle Tony (it's almost always Weird Uncle Tony). Whether it was too much love that smothered him, or not enough that deadened him, or a mutant Neuregulin 1 gene that tried, convicted, and sentenced him from the moment he came into this world and nine months before. Fuck it. The fact of the matter is, he did what he did and paid it forward before he chose to put a bullet in his brain, or that same knife through his own trachea. So, frankly, I don't much care about the story behind it; just how it all ends. And if I had to venture a guess by the way she spat out the aftertaste of his name, Tessa Dunlap Abernathy didn't really give two shits either.

To my utter shock and surprise, the application sailed through. For a week now, that ancient image of my future had embedded in every gray crevice and wrinkle of my brain. With my passport stamped, I went back to the Chrons, paid their pound of flesh, and gave them the address of where to drop my Lockbox ahead of my arrival…along with the recovery fee for after the job was done. Then I put out the fire in my pocket. The only thing left to acquire that was out of my hands was the Artifact. See, tachyons are dumped into the machine's particle accelerator before blasting your lucky ass out into the Ether, and the faster they travel before they throw you your strike, the farther back you're able to go.

So, your destination era is mostly a product of velocity, but we're talking differentials in fractions of a millimeter per microsecond translating to months or years with each teensy bump in acceleration. So, sure, you'll touchdown in the '78, but did you pack enough antique, legal tender to make it for the six months until your mission date arrives? Did you bring enough Senze Tabs to keep you from going insane, when all you've got to live on is a two-dimensional, glass screen blaring something unspeakable called, "The Love Boat" into your eyeballs that seems to have completely bedeviled the masses?

No, jaunts are vacations, not sabbaticals. No Tick in his right mind (your textbook, heavy-breathing Temprophile excluded) would do this job, no matter what the pay, if sitting around navel-gazing in a time before lattes and the Internet (let alone Neuronet) were part of the bargain. So, to make sure jumps are more precise than your average cock-eyed dart throw, you need an "Artifact" assembled as closely to the date that you're shooting for to help the infernal machine better home in. Newspapers are always the best, but once those go extinct, things get trickier until the world gets comfortable enough with data stamping everything to start keeping better records.

The Big Heads say it all relies on a process called "Quantum Entanglement" for the tachyons they've generated in the present to call back to the particles surrounding the Artifact and their original era. Apparently, gluons from one end of Space-Time can interact with gluons on the other, in a way that makes all things connected, preserving the Line and its Fabric. A smarter man might take comfort and even see something beautiful in that; that all things, through all Time, are always connected. But for me, it's more proof of just how fucking weird the world is.

I guess this is why the Chrons and governments don't really worry about people going back. In addition to your poindexter, Kumbaya, "Circle of Life" mumbo-jumbo (which, buy it or not, has brought me back safely from twenty-three chronal displacements—just *two* shy of my free sandwich), unless you've managed to knickknack together your own particle accelerator with spare microwave parts, not many people are gonna be able to "Bill and Ted" around the universe on three-day weekends.

Booking an accelerator, as you can imagine, is a pretty, steel penny, with charges exponentially increasing by the megajoule the farther back you wanna surf. So far, no one's been able to zip tachyons fast enough to send anything back past 1951, as far as the record shows. But, I guess, who's to say some Swedes haven't built a collider the size of Helsingborg underground somewhere and sent their canniest politicians to a front-row seat on someone's face in a Caligulan orgy? But even so, The Timeline stays preserved.

That's probably the biggest reason the Chrons say, "Fuck it!" If it happened, it was our history, so we'd never know the difference; 'cause there was none. "Difference," that is. This is it; what always would have been. Intellectually, the big fear your typical, lefty group or fringe chronologist looking to scrounge up new grant money is gonna squawk on about is someone going back and single-handedly putting their dick somewhere it so absolutely, positively didn't belong that the entire course of human civilization ends up getting spontaneously ear-fucked.

And maybe they're right. Maybe there should be more watchdogs or something a hair more intimidating than a twelve-sheet application process (though, tell me the last time you filled out a paper document *by hand* and then get back to me on how gentle a tickle in the ass that is).   But hell, for all we know, maybe it was an amped out Tick who put one in the Archduke of Austria, or Oswalt was really a joy-jumping, rich dilettante, whose magic bullet didn't originate from a grassy knoll, but four-dimensional space.

But all that said, it's hard to argue with one simple fact: *we're still here*. There's a story; it's the reason why Chrons check for tachyon saturation and little else along the Line— a well-worn parable that both exemplifies and justifies their *unparalleled* (yup, that is absolutely a time pun) laziness. In the early days of jumping, a physicist--one of the pioneers of the tech, which afforded him access--insisted on taking all the risks involved in testing by volunteering himself. For a long time, only a few of his colleagues monitoring the controls knew what he was up to.

Legend goes, he'd grip this old, crumpled up paper swan; crayoned feathers worn and faded along the wings. Then he'd vanish, and reappear instantly (it's how this works). At first, determined for the next jump, and then more withdrawn. Then detached. And then, one time: wet, exhausted, and inconsolable. That was when the alarms must have finally triggered in those oversized craniums that made room to pack in everything but tiny morsels of common sense. They ripped him out of the chair, and someone went back, prying the swan from him once they got him sedated.

Eleven years earlier, on a lake in rural Minnesota, fourteen versions of the physicist blinked in and out of time like spectral fireflies to haplessly watch their eight-year-old son expire on the muddied bank. According to his colleague, there was nothing he could do, no tool he could bring, no faster he could swim, or sooner he could dive…nothing in those fourteen attempts that could save that boy.

And each subsequent copy of the man grew more disoriented: slower, fumbling, and more confused as he witnessed evermore arriving versions of himself fail their son time and time again. According to his coworker, Number Fourteen just sat along the bank, watching, witnessing, *remembering* the scene all at once—for a while completely unsure of which he was and when he'd come from. All the while, the EM bubbles grew more and more unstable as they burst through the air like popped balloons.

In his report, the scientist wrote that he saw waves starting to ripple along the lake's water, indicating the beginnings of a "gravitational anomaly." It was time to go—and never come back. And though it was never exactly a scientifically proven hypothesis, the *emotional* impact of the story was a strong enough psychic jolt to the public consciousness to forever settle the debate. *The past was immutable, and we are, all of us, puppets dancing along invisible strings.*

Turns out Tess had secured a "Have You Seen My Puppy?" ad from the era; one of those things that used to get tacked to the things they used to have to use to make those *other* things they once called "telephones" work. The past is like an alien galaxy, sometimes, I swear. You'd need to see it to believe it. I'm guessing someone took it down to call the pet's owner 'cause they found the thing and then just forgot to toss it. More than half a century later, a relative finds it in their grandpa's storage after he croaks, and suddenly, it might be worth something as news of scientists harvesting elementary particles that can travel back in time has the world all hot and bothered. Or at least, that's what I'm hoping for the doggie's sake, 'cause that's not a case I'm about to fucking take.

It was a lucky find, since the *where*, obviously, is just as important as the *when* for the Artifact. A nickel minted in San Francisco in 1984 doesn't do much good if you've got a job for me in Atlanta, unless you're willing to comp the obscene, ancient travel expenses, along with the small vet's clinic of horse tranquilizers and Quaaludes (AKA: the one thing the past got *right*) it would take to strap me into one of those projectile air-coffins. Last I cracked open my thesaurus, "Rough and Tumble" wasn't yet synonymous with "Suicidal."

But walking into the facility, it was actually my complete lack of anxiety that was notable. I'd been around the block enough times, I figured, but it was always nice to have even a *little* bump of an edge before you start the show. *But not this time.* Maybe it was the reassurance of the photo that had taken all the juice out of it, or maybe it was just that the thrill was gone; I filed that thought to the back of my mind for a future identity crisis. Either way, all of it beats puking like I did my first go-round and forever ruining a five thousand dollar, "Save Ferris!" vintage t-shirt. This time, it'll just be the smell of Axe Body Spray I'll have to acclimate to, which honestly might give my gag-reflex a better run for its money.

But I liked retro Chicago, despite the shitty pizza. Did two jobs there already in '67 and '95. It's better when you know the place—one mystery's enough for your plate. They check my vitals before the final screening. Baseline hypertension. *Thanks, Pop.* I slip back into his shoes and pull up my shorts, abruptly cutting short the nurse's ocular Mardi Gras. That's a joke. "She's" seventeen hundred pounds, and her "eyes" were manufactured by Toshiba. *I'm gonna miss this place.*

As they buckle me in, I notice that they reupholstered the chair since the last time I was here. New cushions. Easier on the neck when things start to shake. I'm grateful. *Sometimes it's the little things.* I stare out at Tess behind the glass and radiation shield while the scientists and lesser creatures scuttle around, but never quite cross within her aura. She's holding the picture.

My mind flashes to another time within this chair. I don't know why. This case...well, this one wasn't rote. Another woman, blonde, hazel eyes, but another Xerox goddess all the same, stormed into my office and embraced me. Not as wonderful a feeling as you'd think when you're ninety percent sure you're having a stroke. Heard I lost an aunt that way—to a stroke, not a beautiful woman's embrace. That'd be how she lost my uncle, and what gave her the stroke in the first place. *We're a classy lot.*

After she stopped shaking, and I got through slapping myself what I deemed a sufficient amount, I eventually pried the story out of her between the Tourette's of "thank-you's". Turns out I saved her on a case, or I would, once she got around to actually hiring me. That's why she was here today—to close the loop. She handed me the business card I'd given her somewhere in her past and in my future. I smirked, and for a brief sec, I was the one shaking; it was eerie to be thanked for a job well done that you hadn't yet decided to do.

She gave me money (technically, payment on services rendered) specifically to go back and help her—sparing her, if not from death, then the thing some find worse. Suddenly, I felt embarrassed about smelling her hair. It was the only time I skipped the background check—probably because the money was good, that card was mine, and no one on Earth is that good of an actress. Though, if there were ever a time to be sure I wasn't getting strung and fleeced, I'm thinking that woulda been it. *Oh well.* A good Tick always leads with his gut, no matter how queasy while walking.

I went back, just a few weeks. She was lucky, really, that paper records had come back in style recently with a culture accustomed to jumping. Her Artifact was a parking receipt. I only had to butcher a few hours, so I had a drink (or three), like a true professional and thought too long about it. For hours, it all came back to one notion…*what if I stayed here drinking?* What in the world and the eternal breadth of the Universe would happen then, if one man sat and nursed his beer?

But I was a Tick, so there was no fundamental force, in this or any other undulating brane, that was gonna prevent me from at least seeing it start—verifying that all this was even true. *That wasn't gonna happen.* Ticks are twelve percent Scotch, eighteen percent severe childhood psychological trauma, and eighty-nine percent curious. We're also mostly undereducated. I had to have a look-see.

I rounded the corner of the alleyway; nothing too ominous, but enough concealment behind the dented, steel dumpster to build a small *Den of Nightmares* if you were determined. As far as I could see, though, it was quiet. She'd given me the time roughly to the minute. You don't forget a thing like that, I suppose, but apparently, I'd actually *instructed* her. My head spun a little, 'til my sights rested on the other side of the crossing. And I thought to myself, deliberately this time: *what if I just walked away?* What if I, alone, by my choosing, defied the Law, both Nature's and Man's, and went about my way? Down my own determined path? *Just who up there could stop me?*

And as I thought these things, I heard the click and scrape of heels worth more than my mortgage before the punctuation of one loud, but muffled, shriek. And I saw my feet--before the cud of those grander, murkier notions had finished its final revolution through my frontal lobe--flying to shove the edge of that dumpster forcefully against the skull of that thing that called itself a man; giving the dumpster one more dent. And just like that, the job was done.

I *de ja vu'd* my past, and her future, as she sprang up, gave the sleeping, oozing thing a kick, and sobbed against me through a fierce, quaking embrace. I stood there, limp as a shiatsued eel carcass against her, trying to process what just happened—to focus in on *the feeling* of whatever it was that got my feet to move before my brain was ready; whatever it was that compelled me, and made me certain, fucked and for all, once I saw it happening, that it was always out of my hands. It was the closest thing I'd ever felt to the hand of Fate. But it was enough.

It was enough to know that something was there, tapping on my shoulder. It was reassuring, and it was terrifying, because I had no real idea where my will stopped and *It* began. Or if even they were, somehow, both just one and the same; the only faces of an intricately cut jewel a darkened light and shittier vision would ever let us see. I never felt a thing like that again, but it was nice to leave it, knowing, somewhere, deep beyond the piled on sediment of cynicism and self-loathing, that I was still on the right end of things, even when I was at rock-bottom. Most importantly, it was the closest thing to definitive proof I could ever hope to get that the old man was full of shit. And that thought reminded me that I had a job to do, and a persona to market.

I calmed her down, fixed her make up, and handed her my card. I could not stress enough how important it was that she find me and remember to tell me about what happened here, and *when*. I gave her the time. She diligently wrote it down, nodding through incrementally smaller gulps of air. It seemed, for some strange reason, she trusted me, and I realized I'd just made the single greatest advertising pitch in human history.

As the chair starts to shake--the metal first--that familiar rattle of the electromagnetic field booting up, Tessa Dunlap

Abernathy stares at me with eyes that say the very same "thank you" for something I've already done, but haven't yet decided to do. In the final microsecond, I drop the cynicism before they dice the atom. *I'm gonna miss this place.*

Electric current bursts all around me, but thankfully, never *through* me. Their coils are kept at bay by the EM field as they outline its invisible, spherical mass with their impotent bluster. *I knew a guy, growing up, like that.* Even with the goggles on, it's more light than I can take, and the earplugs are a joke against the wail of the machine in labor. Still, though, what can only be a trained ear hears the hatch come down from the accelerator tube before the whole word goes white and gone.

The cliché would be that it feels like being born, but Dying feels more appropriate. It's much more a process of being ripped away from all existence than it is of being introduced to the world. Everything, mercifully including your senses, leaves you as the bubble slips from the cliff of the curved edge of Space into some non-place you can't comprehend before snagging the rim of Reality again. *It's one hell of a half-pipe, double backflip.*

And then you land again, softer than you'd expect, at a place back along The Continuum somewhere before your starting line, where it always, for the very first instant of touchdown at least, feels as if that's where you always were; the navigation centers of your brain refusing to buy the laughable, half-baked story your higher functions and memory are trying to force-feed it—that you're a *"Future Man!"* But then, if you can hold your lunch, the next few seconds always prove very critical.

Thankfully, I'm a pro (now one jump away from a free sandwich I'm half sure I could eat during the next jaunt), so upchucking isn't a threat. My head and feet are clear; time for an impact assessment. See, the beauty of the EM is that it protects you, and any incalculably unlucky civilians, from doing too much damage on arrival, same as it did in transit from being ripped to confetti by tachyon bombardment.

The field rebuffs most solid objects to help avoid impact. It also does you the handy solid of preventing ionic phasing— where matter merges with other matter if it jumps into a shared space with an object in the past. *Sounds painful.* So, physically, it's a relatively safe ride, wherever your Artifact dumps you, unless you somehow land over water. Then, I suppose, you are very fucked…but next time, for an Artifact, don't go for the shrimp boat trawl net, maybe?

Now, mentally…that's another issue; the EM's useless there. And it's not so much a problem for you (once you pop your temporal displacement cherry) as it *will be* for the courier who nearly wrecked his fourteen-speed witnessing you materialize into existence from previously empty space. There's no amount of (what is it this era?) salvia that's gonna sufficiently explain *that* away, and no shortage of therapy sessions that will ever stop trying …or charging.

The kid sputters something I can't make out before coming over to me as quickly as his nervous, freaked-the-fuck-out feet will carry him, and I forget I'm still wearing earplugs. He's nice enough to use his novelty size phone to dial for help rather than share a video, and he's taken it pretty easy on the body musk. *He's a good kid.* I reward him with a three-second pulse from my Circulizer just beneath his chin. He drops and wiggles.

I watch for a second to make sure he doesn't chomp his tongue. *Nope.* Small miracles. He's about to feel like he's going into cardiac arrest before he eventually blacks out. It's summer, so I'm hoping the docs will blame it on heat stroke; riding too hard. That'd be enough to cover the "hallucinations." Worst-case scenario, they shove him repeatedly through their big, brain-cancering tube like a hotdog on defrost, trying to bust the ghost of an aneurysm that was never there.

Really, it's a fifty-fifty shot with the overpriced, chicken bone diviners in stethoscopes this era non-sarcastically calls "doctors," but ya know, those odds are good enough for me to walk away in search of a way to make them better…somewhere at the end of a bottle. That's the absolute greatest thing about Chicago—I swear, there's a bar on every block. I double-check to make sure there wasn't a second spotter and flee the scene. He'll be OK. Probably.

They eye my Jansport a little funny, but I can tell it's the kind of bar where they don't ask too many questions. Which is good. Last thing I want is to chat up a stone-sober barkeep with an ear for detail. Too rusty right now for verbal judo at the Olympic level. No, I'm here to listen. And, oh yeah, drink. Jumping always gives me a raging, infanticidal mother of a headache for the first half an hour. Drinking dials it down to something more along the lines of my loopy Aunt Rose. A real bitch, but manageable.

I order a Guinness and a cheeseburger, with minimal slang, and listen to everything but the pounding in my skull— picking up pitch, cadence, vocabulary, and inflection. I skip the accents. I'm not putting on dinner theater; I'm allowed to be from somewhere else, just not *somewhen* else. Besides, these people sound like what some wizard would get if he gave tugboats sentience, which really does wonders for that pounding.

I hear enough after an hour to reach the verdict that the twenty-teens aren't so awful, or rather, could be worse. The 90s were a lot more "out there," with the virus of trendy gibberish infecting the host lexicon, using TV for its primary carrier. *Not to mention all the stupid-ass hats.* I mean, sure, the men here resemble anorexic lumberjacks that specialize in clearing off-map, micro-forests, and some of the women intentionally aim to look like Amazonians who quit when they heard about the part with the boob (I suppose something about global warming in this period severely heats just one half of the head.) But fashion is every generation's Albatross, I've discovered; seems the first hints of decorum and general self-awareness don't manifest in the human psyche until somewhere around fifty.

Most of my pals here are probably a bit more self-aware than they'd care to be, and are making active efforts to fix that. To escape. I don't dwell too long on any personal poignancy there; I've got my own distractions. *Christ, I've missed trans-fats.* I'm wiping a bright, pink mix of Heinz and Hellmann's off my stubble when, suddenly, I'm thrown into a sparring qualifier with an opponent more worthy than the bartender.

My repugnant, trademark snark aside, there are elements to this era that I'll admit to finding somewhat intoxicating, and one of those elemental, primal distractions just took the free seat right next to me. I don't try to read too much into it other than opportunity, and in the back of my head, an annoying little voice I quickly seek to bind, anchor, and drown, starts to question my real reason for being here.

I won't deny that there's an unquestionable appeal to the women in these times. In one word, it's *variety*. The differences, flavors, and options of size, style, and body-type--the visual panorama of perfect imperfection--it's like first seeing color, and enough to make your head spin and your parts pound worse than any jump. Believe me. When you come from a world full of machine-minted copies as your gold standard, and a widening class of hoi polloi clawing to be their funhouse reflection via installment plan, you sorta forget how Nature originally planned things out. I guess, unlike fashion, a misogynistic Patriarchy has held pretty steady through the ages, but it's just nice to experience a time when you couldn't pay a price to have all its tenants so perfectly enforced—all the way down to the genome.

She breaks the ice by asking what I'm drinking. I'm secretly a little sore about the missed opportunity. My line woulda been a hell of a lot more interesting. It's the first I've heard of the brand, but my pronunciation holds. My toes start to tingle. There's that thrill; better late than never. Clearly, I'm a drunken savant. I offer her a round and start "shaking off the cobwebs." I pretend that I'm getting practice in at blending in; that this will help the mission; that I haven't done this a hundred, a thousand, a hundred thousand times before; that this isn't second-nature -truer nature- but it's as much a game with myself as the one I play with her.

It was always this way, with people of any era—a thing I probably owe more to my father than my bar tab. If I hear the song once, I can play it, right on cue; it's not a challenge of can I do it, but how quickly, how effectively, and how deeply she'll believe it. I run through all the options in my head as I improvise, this time donning the pliable skin of a consumer protection advocate, not quite sure if that's partly true or not (or even, honestly, a completely real thing), but I find it suitably creative, and an outfit I've never worn before. I push my backpack under my stool.

The thrill holds steady, but finding the rhythm happens too easy. As I keep her hydrated, I whet her appetite for more with predictions, knowledge, and theories of things never before spoken in the world that exponentially broaden her addled, primitive mind (and her bank account, if she'd pay enough attention,) giving her a solid, four-star collegiate lecture of a semester's worth of material in under an hour. Suddenly, I feel a little less bad as I consider that buying her free beer is a hell of a refinanced tuition price.

But that was the issue. It wasn't the booze-based numbness, now well on to conquering my fingertips; all that helped me do was to think of it less. *The truth.* That who she was, where she was from, what she wanted to be, and even what she was saying to me at this very, single second; none of it mattered a good goddamn to me more than the cut of her dress and its willful determination to ride slowly up her bare thigh.

I look around as her words slur out to ears that might as well stayed plugged, and cast my verdict. They were not, a single one of them, real people; they were ghosts, all long dead. Being here, to me, was like walking through one of those cardboard suburbs they made for atomic testing— strolling along a defunct era as the only actual living thing for an experiment of the atom all my own.

I was not a part of it; any of it. I was beyond. I could tip the tables. I could punt the plastic dog. Set fire to the hand-sewn drapes, already all destined to go up in flames. I could do to them whatever I wanted without any consequence as far as I, or anyone who would one-day matter, could tell. This entire world is my playground. I'm not just king of the mountain; I am God.

Then, that amber tide breaks, and obscene, private notions recede once again into the depths of the subconscious, where they belong, and I realize, for a second, that was the closest I would come to understanding Ryan Cooper Hanes. *I make sure of it.* She drapes her arm around me, mistaking my quivering for being cold, rather than a little more dead, and I order us a final round to help us figure out a way to more efficiently drown our sorrows and slay loitering demons. Thankfully, she didn't live too far away.

I told myself I needed it as much as she did; at least that wasn't a lie. Maybe I'd officially hit my limit on those; the account closed from too much withdrawal activity. *Maybe I'm just an asshole.* I watch her as she sleeps and I dress, and I acknowledge I've done worse; to women and these phantom, cardboard people, that is. I think the ridiculous thought of the kid still there, writhing over asphalt, and I pray that nobody took his bike.

There were times when I had to, *chose to*, leave less elegantly. "Just-in-case" drugs, which I still carry, that you can drop in a drink, or shove directly down an esophagus. They turn you into a ghost; make you disappear like something that was never there, and they'll lose about an hour for every milligram. Never felt good about those, but that's the job, and you're not a God as much as a sideshow magician; nothing more than another man behind another curtain.

Sometimes you drink too much, and you slip up and say something that can compromise you past the game's playful point -to one of no return- until they catch the scent and won't let up 'til the truth is snared between their teeth and dragged out screaming for the world to see while you're left forever blowing bubbles in a sanitarium. Or you leave your bag to take a leak, and she's playing with a HoloTell phone; you can't just say you, "got it from Japan." Or, more likely than all the rest, the drug's just easier than telling someone an empty, pointless thing like, "goodbye." You choose to keep it professional.

She snores a little below me while I finish buttoning my shirt. She's out completely; not sure how much of that is me and how much was the tap. I look on the floor as if I'm leaving something behind, the notion scratching persistently against some spot on my brainstem, but without any picture coming clear. It's annoying. I scan around for Dad's shoes. Was that it? They don't fit well; snug. Maybe my feet have swollen. Alcohol can really fuck up your body; Pop could tell you that better than anyone.

The night air is refreshing enough that you forget it's toxic in this backwards time when vehicles sputtered out more fumes than tire fires. Regardless, I need to cool down. I try not to think too hard about the fact that I can't remember her name already. In the morning, that will be a blessing. I check my pack. I'm pretty good on era tender. Coulda brought more to be safe; tracking that shit down is a real rabid gerbil up your ass. Only a few brokers I can trust won't give me counterfeit (not worth the risk from the things I've heard about prison these decades, since I'm pretty satisfied with my colon at its current circumference), and Dennis was giving me a real bullshit exchange rate a week ago. So much for customer loyalty; the prick. And though I obviously cover local currency as part of my service fee, why rip the Doll off just to fatten The Menace's pocket?

No, the better move is to bring something relatively (or undetectably, at least) timeless to pawn after touchdown. Not timeless as in expensive, but timeless as in its era of origin isn't consequential, or identifiable. Shit they still make the same way in the future; silverware, clocks, jewelry; that kind of thing. She handed me a pearl necklace, and I told her that would do. I won't lose nearly as much in conversion if I swap it here and now, but I assured her it was only for emergencies, and that she'd more than likely see it back; even wrote her up a little insurance card to prove I wasn't full of it. Better safe than stranded. I'm tracking a maniac, remember, so you never know if a sudden plane ticket (ugh) or surgery (first one's still worse) might be in order.

I keep it in my Lockbox, which I go to check on for the first time since drop-off. Still intact; maybe not quite a third of the way full. *Ha, the things you'll see.* I place the necklace inside, and then I remember having seen it here before. Despite myself, I caught glimpses of it on other jumps a few years out, and closer to my future. It's kinda hard to miss; nice to know it doesn't get stolen, and that I won't have to pay that insurance. I'd always wondered why it was there and who it really belonged to. Well, now I know, and I'd say finding out was worth the wait. I chalk that up as another case closed before I do the same for the Lockbox and set the combination. *Numbers...how quaint.*

A lot of people ask me, if you can time-shift, why bother doing any kind of job at all? Why not just open an account in 1959 and collect your interest/lottery ticket in the present? Well, not a bad proposition, but the Chrons are two steps ahead of you. They're monitoring everything on the Line, especially that which involves the hint of a scent of a rumor of money. If you leave a given account, untouched for too long, it becomes forfeit. And guess who gets to collect? So yeah, even if you're here on pleasure, you better at least pretend to have some business, or the Chrons will sniff you out, and your trip to the Past won't end up being very much of either. Oh, and don't even get me started on trying to smuggle something away on the return trip…

By now, I'm sick of walking. I choose some place small and tucked away, partly 'cause it's cheap, partly 'cause it's nowhere, and mostly because it makes me feel like a PI. The more busted letters on the "MOTEL" neon, the better. It's tradition, and you can only get the authentic experience on these jumps, in these eras. I pay cash, and they don't bat an eye. "ID" is a foreign word. Perfect. Ha, for all I know, the place is another form of cash trap run by Chrons, but I don't care. I just need a bed without another body.

I wake up with a fire in my chest in the middle of the night. I can't swallow stale air quick enough. Nice. My pillow's drenched. I claw for my bearings, and come up empty-handed. Jetlag. Normally, the first night post-transit, I get disoriented and wake up thinking I'm still in my apartment—in my old bed, in my own time; the real time, which still marches on somewhere without me. A more civilized, but far less interesting world. But this time; this time, I am sure I'm back at her place; that I was sleeping there the entire time. I quickly, and even more quietly, show myself the door, only to find myself stepping over the face of a consumer protections advocate from Ohio. It was the skin of the person I'd shed and left behind.

I understood and admitted, maybe consciously for the first time (since this jump, at least) why I was really here; longing for a roach motel I was so certain I deserved. Each time, I somehow think it will be different; that a light will flick on called Virtue -its switch mounted to that itchy part in the back of my mind- and all will be as right as rain. I'll do this for the client, for Justice, for the world, and for the Line. And not for me.

But that was the dream, and now I was awake, drowning in my own sweat. My eyes were open and, the only thing I saw there in that room with me was the Truth: that every time I go back is a chance to start over; for a new beginning, and a new me. Whoever I want to be, whoever I could have been and should have been back in the place where and when it mattered; in the real world, not this dead facsimile. I was all those things here—on a whim. In an instant. In this place, with each trip, I was every possibility and anything I dared set my imagination on. Anything but me.

That was the vacation. That's why I left. On a job, when I go back, all I was, and am, or ever failed to be doesn't exist, because here, it hasn't happened yet. Here, I'm never really me. It was never them I wanted to control; that I needed power over. That was the story of a man somewhere out there with three names and four victims. No, it was, and always has been, about me. And the next morning, I was going to wake up, put on my shoes, and prove that. Tomorrow, I would start the hunt.

The next morning, I don't think too hard about the subject of my investigation. There's nothing I can do. If I had found anything out, I would have passed the info to the Conventionals when I handed Hanes over for the arrest. But I know I don't, because, in the future, he remains unidentified. So, what's the point investigating? Probably someone they discover back at whatever subterranean cave this beast calls a home, body too decomposed to lift any records. Or maybe just a hapless vagrant. Who knows? It's completely out of my hands. Thankfully, though, I've got a better lead.

Marjorie Janice Brown. The second victim. Body discovered at 4:55 PM later today around the intersection of North Dearborn and West Ontario. I realize now that I'm pacing; I only do that when my Tick's gut has indigestion. All my logic centers know it's futile, but I strongly consider slapping away Fate's nagging hand from its perch, thrumming a rhythm across my shoulder. I don't know; something's recently stirred in me. I make the call, and my stomach settles. My shoulder's free. I'll get there early; a stakeout. No matter how many hours I have to wait, I'm going to try to get the jump on this bastard, and save Marjorie's life.

I load up with everything I've got: helioflares, EMPulsers, delirials, racket-rounds, magbinds, and my handy, dandy circulizer. He's Jack the Ripper, and I'm a goddamn Jedi. Again, no need to pull a mental muscle figuring out his next moves; I know them all. I switch off and sufficiently stash my telesponder, which helped brake my pacing by granting me access to anything ever broadcast in this year. They may be a lot of warmongering, homophobic, planet-killers…but they damn sure know how to TV—even without emphonics. I boot up my map, double-lock the door, and officially punch the clock. The chase is on. I thank my lucky stars my target's name is Ryan Cooper Hanes, and not Walter White.

I may apprehend serial killers, but my work itself isn't too exciting. The cross-streets are a twenty-four minute bus ride out from the motel, and the only trick to the rest is not getting spotted as I set up shop; future tech has its disadvantages that way. It's something of a busy intersection, which comes as a surprise to me given that it's about to be the location of an alleged, future homicide, in broad daylight, no less. It takes fifteen minutes for the coast to clear and give me an opening. I don't need much; my metamaterial blanket does the work for me.

I switch on the current, and my skin turns to brick, at least to anyone walking by. I clear out of the way of foot-traffic, hunker down, and try my hardest not to sneeze for the next four hours. I could have brought a few Senze Tabs, but I need to stay sharp. I spend the bulk of my time trying to figure out how Skyler's gonna react when she finally meets Heisenberg as I wager all my hopes, dreams, and Marjorie's life on the full potential of the original uncertainty principle.

Three hours and fifteen minutes later, I have my answer. Right on time. At 4:41 PM, Marjorie Brown heads down Ontario toward me. I power it down and rip off my cloaking blanket, not really giving three-quarters of a fuck who sees me. The hairs rise along my neck, and I roll two, live racket-rounds nervously in my right hand's palm. I'm ready for everything.

I'm already time sensitive, and the seconds tick away like hours, especially at the pace she's moving. Walking in heels is not her strong suit. She has a gingerly, hobbling gait, and she's tugging at her waistband awkwardly. I can't imagine being a woman. I scan around, and the street is empty. So far, so good, until she nearly slips on something wet that wasn't there before. Oh God.

He didn't do it here; this is just where they found her. I check my watch. 4:43 PM. Marjorie Brown takes her final step before collapsing across the pavement. I race to her with lead feet in mocking loafers more than reluctant to go and verify the truth. My shoulders are heavy once again.

She struggles to keep her gaze on me against more convincing protest from her eyelids. Still, she somehow finds a way to extend a hand and unfurl three fingers out to me. I stare at them and then take a big step backwards from the swelling puddle she's spilled beneath her. I can't touch her. I can't help. I can't be anywhere near this, because I was never here. I patch into the emergency dispatch feed to reroute all drivers directly, but I'm riding out a loser's hand. A lateral incision at least six inches deep into the abdomen. He gutted her.

I want to give her something: comfort, assurance, that goddamn picture; any proof at all that the monster that savaged and mutilated her won't get away. But all I can convey is rage, and that isn't what she needs. She closes her eyes and enters the darkness alone; all parts of me shaking against a desire to fuck the rules, wade into her agony, and hold her tight until it's done. It's the only thing I want, save for the guy's head as an antique conversation piece, but I can't risk giving it to her. The muscles in those fingers slacken and fall as I resign to failing her again. Maybe it's a side-effect of one dip too many into the Time-stream, but I think I hear Fate chuckle slightly as it cuts away her strings.

No, it's the sirens; they're my cue. Until, that is, I clock a flash of movement from the corner of my eye. Down the street, one hundred feet ahead, he stares at me, and I don't have to see him to know that he's smiling; I can feel it in my bones. I shudder, more from the flare of a white-hot, vengeful wrath than the primal anger that a thing like that shares 99.9 percent of my DNA. He lingers more than he should; high, drunk, and more than likely engorged by the sight and ramifications of his handiwork. He listens to the symphony's crescendo. They're almost here.

A crosswalk sign changes across the street, and I need to be gone. He still watches, wondering what I'll do. My one advantage is that I know everything about him, but for Ryan Cooper Hanes, I'm a defect puzzle piece; a total mystery, and most certainly not part of the plan. I update my ample database on him by stealing a quick sample from Marjorie with my biometric analyzer. His DNA will be all over it, which means that I will be all over him. I feel that once-chilling smile fade completely. He doesn't like that.

I let him evaporate into the sea of bodies flooding the crosswalk; actively coursing with Life. *They must all profoundly offend him.* My thinking's simple; I don't want to startle my prey and send him running out of state at the sight of my Comforter of Invisibility. It's torturous and frustrating, but I let my gut make the call. This is the action I would take, and it will lead me to him. I leave Marjorie Brown alone again, stepping slowly to quiet my father's shoes. I cannot look back. The EMTs with their kit of thumbtacks, glue, and Popsicle-sticks arrive just in time to meet a freshly dead woman. I'll let them figure out an introduction.

I head back to the motel. For a moment, I wonder if that was premeditated or a crime of random opportunity. *The thoughts of a real detective.* The kind of thoughts that will drive you insane. I find my keycard and quickly shake them away. It was not having to entertain thoughts like those that made me pick being a Tick -a cheater- in the first place. I don't need to be them; all I have to do is hunt.

Problem is, I don't have a lead now. The bio-analyzer was a good move. I separate his DNA signature (Caucasian, male, Type 1 diabetic) from Marjorie's and what must be her dog's; Cairn Terrier. I assume it's hers; doubt an animal would last long around him. The green light flashes; it accepts his scent. If he comes within five miles of the machine's molecular scanners, it will go off, and sniff him out. It will lead me right to him.

But Marjorie was the last victim whose records were available. I don't know anything about his next move 'til some douche's cellphone snaps that pic that will send me treading a hole along this bile-stained carpet. And that

doesn't happen for another two days. Two days; alone.
Well, never alone; not with that voice chiming in loud and
clear. It's the next day, and as foretold, I've forgotten her
name, but there's one name the voice won't let me shake:
Marjorie Janice Brown. Marjorie Janice Brown. Marjorie
Janice Brown.

Before I know it, my heels hang on a barstool, and my head
swims in rye. Well, not my head, I tell myself; this isn't
me. But I don't tell her—her body softer and dress shorter
than the first. I tell her lots of things, but the ones that
matter are never true. My pace is better this time, and her
apartment's smaller.

I lose track of the days, the time, the masks, and the women.
It's all a blur—a rolling, congealed mass. A libertine
hurricane; a blank slate. A new bed. A new me. But just
like that persona, it's all pretend. Counterfeit. And I know,
in the back of my mind, in the words of that screeching
voice, that when the vacation's over, and this world is
stripped away in a particle tidal wave, I'll have to deal with
just myself again, and all the same questions always left
unanswered. Those dark, internal mysteries I'm far too
shitty an imposter PI to ever solve…at least, 'til the next
gig. *Or is it the next fix?* What was I saying about those
Tachyon Thirst fucks again?

Somewhere in the eye of the storm, Marjorie's name
becomes just that again: a name, and not a regret. For a

while, I cower under the shroud of a false skin, already fraying in preparation to be peeled away; its purpose through. My shoes wait empty for me, and I think of my father.

One time, when I was young, and one world was more than I could take, my father took a belt to me. Real, farm-grown leather with a stainless steel clasp. He thought, I'm sure, he was beating something out of me by venting all his self-loathing away with the skin over my back, but the truth is, all he was really doing was beating the worst parts of himself into me. I think, somewhere deep down, in a place he hid from everyone, and himself most of all, he knew it, and it only made him hate himself more, so the cycle kept on churning.

Its revolutions ended abruptly one day on a hospital bed that had grown accustomed to his shape in the final month. Cirrhosis. Could have easily cultured him a liver (I had the money), but he was one of those extreme, Church of Luddite technophobes. "A real man accepted his destiny," he would say. I think his thumb was on the scale, giving Destiny a hand. He wasn't a man built for his time. I tell her the ER needs me and make my escape. I repent for it by warning her not to fly Malaysian any time next near. I guess I am my father's son.

In a few hours, Ryan Cooper Hanes will be in custody, and I hope I'll hate myself less. But I'll be home, so I know that won't be true; the vacation isn't over yet. Tess may have spoiled the ending, but the best stories are all about the journey there. Guess I know that path now too, thanks to my literal and mechanical bloodhound. This time, I'm not about to wait around by some cross-streets for him to arrive at his predestination. I know where he's heading, so I'll search and track him, and when he steps foot anywhere within the radius of my five-mile net, I'll spring the trap. Just before I give him to the cops, his ass will be mine.

I stalk around the area, eyes glued to an impossible doodad I pray no one gives a second look. Thankfully, their sights are all too hypnotized by their own archaic technology to notice me, or much of the world around them. I guess we're all on the run from Reality. It's little comfort, but the time is now. I need to face my own, and think about my steps for heading back.

First is the Lockbox. Once I have Hanes filed and processed, I'll need to leave a note inside telling Tess when to grab me and snap me back; a necessary move for any jumper who wants to muck around in the Past more than a few minutes, like the old days. They'll activate another Tachy squall and EM bubble on their end (using the note for a kind of reverse-Artifact) and poof, I'm back in the chair, typically not seconds after I've disappeared. The lab boys will have missed one hell of a three-day bender.

In this scheme, the security and, well, continued existence of the Lockbox are key. In the most basic terms, it's a locker; portable, and stored in a place guaranteed enough to last a few centuries without anyone fucking with it. For a not-so-small fee, the Chrons guard (and also stash) the lot of them to help lower the risk of vagrants and stranded SOBs along the Line. *Keep business moving.* For now, in this time, it's just a combination lock, but on the other end, I've had it biometrically upgraded. I program a client's thumbprint and voice sig, and the door will open when they need to grab the "OK, get me the fuck out of here" message after the job is done. When I get back, I delete their access. Easy-peasy. This allows me to keep multiple jobs active, even as I hopscotch eras. Only problem is trust.

A Tick has to buy that a client (who, let's face it, you're putting your whole existence on the line, heh, with anyway) will only take the message meant for them and leave the ones accumulating for future jobs alone. It's certainly something to think on (with only occasional, cold night-sweats), but why risk getting yourself on the Chrons' shit-list over some damn scrap of paper? You'd really have to fucking hate me (not an impossible feat) to implicate yourself so obviously. It's got your bio-data in there for Christ's sake; fuck a smoking gun. Though, I guess if you're committed, it's a hell of a lavish murder-suicide.

Back home, I haven't looked in on my box in a while, but it was nice to know when I first bought it that I'd have a sweet, little career; opening it up to find it stuffed to the gills with envelopes. But I never looked at them. Ever. Know some guys who did leaf through and study all of theirs; learn their futures. Never ended well. I check every week and before each jump to see that it's there, though. *So far, so good.* Somewhere far beyond the temporal horizon, Tess is gripping a retrieval note I haven't yet written. I can't help grinning like some idiot kid. I guess it's comforting having a guardian angel.

Still nothing on the scanner. I make a right and try east of the final rendezvous. Won't be long now. We're thirty minutes out. After I deliver the note, the pick-up prep follows. The motel will do; I still have the room for the full day. It's always the same routine: "shower," search, and suit up, then back into the clothes I wore on arrival. Helps the tachyons get a bead, they say. Seems it's much easier to send things back to their original time than out of synch. Apparently, the Line likes to preserve its natural order. Doubt the clothes are that big a deal, though. What is important, *damn fucking important*, is that you come in clean. It's what I was saying before; you electron pulse shower to get as many era-particles off you as possible, bombarding yourself with quantum elements from the present stored in the "showerhead." I suspect that's the bigger deal, particularly in helping to snatch you then, as opposed to the moment the retrieval note was written. But I just work here; don't ask me how they make the soup.

Then comes the search. Anything era-contemporary with a mass over half a gram will get you in trouble, and anchor you down to your current period. Like a dead weight, it will rip through your EM field and more than likely take a chunk of you with it. Knew a guy who "left" (or so he says) an era penny in his ass pocket. It's true, though; who ever checks those things? Arrived back in the chair bloody and wailing. The damn thing had fused into his big toe. And it's still there. Only upside is he'll never need tap shoes. So, moral of the story, I'll have to remember to give some time for prep and a double-check. And for Tess, ideally, a shave.

First thing's first, though. The analyzer puts him at a third of a mile away; its signal will take me right to him. Question is, is this business or pleasure? Did I happen to nab him out buying more mini-marshmallows for his homemade Rice Krispies Treats (AKA the one other thing redeeming thing about this era,) or is out pursuing his calling? After two torturous days laying low following our blinking contest, is he here, now, to make another "masterpiece"? Either way, I'm gonna guess he brought his brush; that six to ten inch, collapsible, serrated blade he painted Marjorie Brown red with. But that's fine by me. As I pick up speed, I'm not the least bit intimidated, 'cause in my pants, I'm packing an arsenal.

I hit a right. There's a cluster of pedestrians up ahead; tourists mostly, but also a fair collection of business types nearly mowing people over to make Lunch. *He couldn't pick off one of them?* Then I zero on him, and regret my joke. He's in the thick of the pack, and I know exactly what he's doing: reconnaissance. Choosing the next "still life." He's finding his prey. As I slowly approach, my breath growing labored and muscles drawing tight -that resurrected thrill now cresting in violent, coursing waves through every cell and protein within my body- I can't duck the thought that there's a reason I can read him like a comic book; that maybe we are just one and the same.

Fuck. That thought's enough to distract me into straying too close. In a skyscraper's glass, he catches my reflection. He doesn't bolt, not yet, not in this thicket of people/victims/objects/vessels/ghosts; whatever he sees them as. He's too smart; too practiced at avoiding attention. He'll wait for a clearing, then hit the gas. *But I'm pretty skilled at what I do too, Ryan, so I'm at the starting line whenever you're ready.*

The signal over 14th Street flashes to "Walk," and he doesn't quite obey. He takes off like a vactrain with a half-a-block head start; faster than my guesses gave him credit for, but as my loafers grind pavement, I'm not worried. He's fast, but only for his subspecies, and I've taken all my future vitamins.

I corral him just before I try to overtake him. *Remember, I know where this is going.* I block him from a right turn and consult the analyzer's holomap. We make a violent birth out onto South Morgan to a warm welcome of large eyes and just-extending fingers. Perfect. The din of commotion rising from our wake streams by in an impressionist, peripheral blur. My eyes are only on one target. I can see the station up ahead, and he isn't slowing down. Almost there.

I shut down the map and stow the machine. With the attention of the crowd, it's better to go analog than digital - knuckles over tech- and give the woman what she paid for. *"Rough and Tumble," right?* I move to overtake him, done with the ruse that this was a contest he could ever win; Fate's hand moving from my shoulder to shove me in the back for an extra boost of speed. I reach out for his flaring jacket, when something bright glares harsh against my eyes. The loafers stumble. His paintbrush. Getting an up-close view once my vision returns, I see it's much closer to ten inches than six.

We're heading for another crowd, up on Maxwell; the conventional's station right on that corner. I don't know why, but he doesn't seem to care. He has to know. He's from this area; he's stalked these streets. It's his hunting ground. So, why?

And then, I'm him again. Like a real Dick, for a change. I see 20/20 through his vision; I finally have my answer. The victims were, all of them, crimes of passion. Spur of the moment opportunity. Divine Intervention, and unto him, it has been delivered once again. He's found his prey; a young girl at the back of the street traffic who can't be more than fourteen. I don't know her name, or her blood type, or a single goddamn thing about her. Including how she makes it out of this.

He knows this is the end, and he doesn't give a soggy shit. Doing it before the cops will only magnify his glory. He's ready for the world to see, and I'm giving him his spotlight. All he wants is a grand finale. All he wants is her.

She can't hear me scream above the passing conversation of ugly, combustion engine crates zooming down Maxwell. The way he stares at her -eyes hungry and lustful for a final, carnal bite of their last meal- there wasn't anything in my pocket now that I was certain could put him down without leveling the block; the crowd was just too close.

She was closer. *Seconds now.* He really was faster than I imagined. His instrument flashed toward its unmarred canvas much quicker than I could ever hope to stop it. But any PI worth half his shit knows every problem has its solution, and every mystery, somewhere out there, has an answer; all you have to do is look hard enough to see it.

And I did look, right at her, and in that immortal second, I knew I didn't have to worry about dropping a pick up note into an empty Lockbox. Just like the time in the alley with the dumpster and its second dent, when a Tick's unstoppable, intrinsic curiosity got the better of me. Once I saw her, it was never a question; there was only ever one way this could end.

I yank, hard, back on his billowed coattail to swerve the blade, and that smile slowly finds his face again when he feels the weapon meet its hilt inside of me. He drags it right a little, through most things vital, and twists in an effort to pull free and continue lighting up the scoreboard. But I hold his hand steady and return the blade right back into the scabbard; back to rest in a place of physical pain that, in all my travels, I had no Earthly idea could ever possibly be real. I smile right back at Ryan Cooper Hanes. I trust my gut.

Over his shoulder, right on cue, his would-be final victim, that fourteen-year-old girl, finally takes notice of her surroundings to scream, and dash away far into the safety of the alerted crowd. *This is gonna be good.* With my trained detective's eye, I look everywhere on Hanes's face for a lingering trace of that smile. I come up empty.

He cries "uncle" and drops the weapon before making a desperate, final scramble for freedom, and the chance to slay another day. I'm still smiling; I know he won't get it.

The little girl has signaled a quartet of officers by now. They seem to take her tears and frantic screeching seriously. He can't push through the curtain of sacrilegious, breathing bodies fast enough for another footrace. He tries to fight, but he's nothing without his accomplice. It's a shitty craftsman that blames his tools.

They take him down in under four seconds. I stumble forward for a closer look. The little girl can't find me in the thickening crowd. They snap the bracelets and begin to haul him away in a sight I've seen some place and time before. I look down on a pair of ruined shoes. *How's that for being a man?* Someone finds the knife, and they start unfurling yellow tape. A clamor rises from the converging gawkers, but just above it, I hear the obnoxious click of an imaginary, digital shutter, and I can't help but wonder if maybe that's the one. *Guess that's a mystery I won't get around to.* My head spins like before a jaunt, but I'm thinking I'll stay right here. My legs back me up by giving out beneath me. I drop my arm and let the five-inch hole in my stomach (or, my new bellybutton), get some air. It gurgles out a thank-you.

Then someone steps into the light to darken my vision even further. With all that's left, I force my head to tilt a fraction. Turns out, it's worth it, and I immediately stand corrected as I gaze upon a thing of pure radiance, too impossibly brilliant for this bleak time. Tessa Dunlap

Abernathy, *Tess*, looks down at me with eyes that still say, "thank you." She wears her pearl necklace I had left behind just to make Perfection manifest, and I wish I'd gotten in that shave. At least now I know what to say "you're welcome" for.

I want to apologize as she ruins her shoes to wade into the evidence of my conclusion, but she doesn't seem to care. She breaks our gaze for a very swift moment to look back at Hanes disappearing from existence into the station, and I'm honored, in that instant, to witness her face; it was nice to leave knowing that I was still on the right end of things; it was nice to know here, at the end, that someone was out there waiting for me. With me. All along.

I extend three fingers out to Tess, and she takes my hand. As she crouches down, I stare back at her and allow myself to drown completely in those two emerald whirlpools instead of the warm, metallic tide ebbing in my throat. As her tears fall to purify the murky pool below, I wonder if she knew about the unidentified man the entire time, and how that must have been for her to send me on my mission.

My hand slackens in her grip, and my eyes close. I can't take the swelling light. She calls my name, but my ears are plugged now thanks to all the racket. I feel it; a thrill all through me, down to every quark, just like a Tachy swarm coming to rip me away, and she knows.

She knows I have to go alone…

One last trip…

One last case…

And one final mystery on the other side…

I wonder…

I wonder what I'll find?

The Nuremburger Trial

by Mark Daponte

Scott F. Willard sat on his jail cell's cot and waited for the prison guard to take him to the courthouse, where he would hear a lawyer try to convince a jury that he was an accomplice to mass murder.

"It's not fair. I was just an actor—acting as a company's spokesman," Scott thought. "Since when does acting deserve a death sentence? Well, maybe if you're a real bad actor. But I was good! Maybe too good. But—"

Scott knew he could only fool himself and not any jury, for if being guilty was a math formula, he and his co-conspirator, Sam Jefferson, were guilty squared. Any lawyer's words could never let a jury forget the men's incriminating words that were surreptitiously recorded by the FBI:

"C'mon, Scott. You're more than my company's pitchman. I look at you as an older brother to me who, who knows w-w-when—"

"Hold on. Whenever you stammer, I know something's eating at you. Are you worried about anyone being on to your money laundering? Is that why you're a little, uh, n-n-n-nervous?"

"It's not that. I'm stammering because I got word from one of our meat processing facilities that a batch of burgers was mistakenly sent out. The mistake and now problem is, this batch tested positively for E-coli."

"Hold on. When you say a 'batch,' how many burgers are you talking about?"

"Around fifty."

"God, Sam! That's awful! E-Coli is not good P.R."

"For some other company and country, maybe, but not mine."

"What do you mean?"

"I mean that bad batch won't be eaten in America. See, the meat processing plant was in Sioux City, Iowa, and 99.9% of its, ahem, 'batches' get shipped to China."

"Great! If it winds up there, we can blame *their* unsanitary food handlers and not our meat processing plant, like we did for that last e-coli outbreak in Pakistan."

"Exactly! And I know I don't have to say this, but all this information is strictly confidential. If word got out that we have ten pounds of bad burgers, we'd have to throw away 50 tons of beef."

"Mum's the word, Sam. Our jobs are to sell billions of burgers, not lose billions of dollars. I, uh, guess."

"Good. But, um, why the 'n-n-n-nervous' face, Scott?"

"Just thinking. What if the '99.9% odds' that it gets shipped to China—what if those odds aren't in our favor? And the bad batch winds up in America?"

"Hey. Even if it does kill a few Americans, I'd rather have fifty people go down for good than have McRonald's stock go down temporarily."

"I agree. Losing fifty fatties is better than losing billions of dollars."

Fifty people didn't wind up dying. But 39 people from a single McRonald's restaurant in Schaumburg, IL lost their lives. And 39 people would still be alive if Sam Jefferson or Scott Willard did what they believed was unthinkable: put people's lives over their company's profits.

"What was done, was done," Scott said as he paced his cell. "Now it's time; time for me to suffer the consequences. But first…"

Scott reached under his bedframe, removed a flat cardboard box containing his "Donald McRonald" costume and giddily put on his old work clothes. Against his lawyer's advice that he'd be making a mockery of the court and "sticking it to the judge and jury," Scott decided he'd wear his company clothes at his trial. He felt that if he was going to go down, he'd go down "wearing the uniform of his company's ship."

He sighed and his throat tightened. After a quarter of a century of playing Donald McRonald, just seeing the colors yellow and red next to each other still made Scott grow goose pimples, and occasionally leak tears of pride and joy.

Scott didn't look at himself as a 58 year old guy in a clown suit. As he told his ex-wife: "I'm not just any clown; I'm *the* Donald McRonald, a beloved, instantly recognizable icon, and more popular than Jesus Christ. After all, way more people go to a McRonald's to get fed than go to a church to feed their pathetic souls."

Scott would put his undying allegiance to McRonald's on public display by having a 5' x 5' flag made of himself dressed as Donald McRonald, standing against a yellow and red striped background. Each morning, he'd run the "Donald McRonald flag" up his front yard's flagpole and salute it as if "McRonald Land" was his native country. He would follow this up by singing the McRonald Land national anthem:

"You deserve a break today, so get up and get away, to McRonald's!"

Scott loved everything about the job, from slapping on white grease paint, a red striped shirt, red wig, size 45 shoes, and rubber nose, to:

- visiting a Donald McRonald House and trying to make kids with cancer laugh.

- going on "Toy Tours;" which meant traveling across America and handing out movie tie-in toys to children in McRonald's indoor "Playland's."

- handing out diplomas to graduates of "Hamburger State University;" a training facility for restaurant managers in Tree Brook, Illinois.

Yes, Scott knew he was different than the "average American." Most loved smelling coffee brewing in the morning; he loved the scent of hamburgers grilling in the afternoon.

"Yeah, guess I'm a company man all the way—all the way to the gas chamber. Oh well. There's worse ways of dying. Like eating only organic food," he mused as he put on his oversized shoes. He wiped away tears, looked at the camera pointing towards his cell and thought, "There's worse ways to die than eating an e-coli burger. Like eating this!"

He ripped open the sole of his left shoe, pried two fingers in a carved out hole and removed a capsule filled with yellow powder. Scott crushed it between his teeth, weakly saluted, then whispered, "Long live McRonald Land!"

***

As the prison guard unlocked the cell, Scott Willard's eyelids slowly closed.

***

When Scott opened his eyes, he faced a Jersey cow standing on its back hooves and dressed in an ash gray three-piece suit. Scott smiled and thought, "That is one hell of a cow costume. Wow! Wait…"

Is it a costume?

As part of his Donald McRonald job, Scott personally visited stockyards and smelled a cow's hide up close; what stood before him had the same odor, which was a combination of methane mixed with dated hay.

"And this actor in the cow suit—he smells the same," Scott thought. "No. That doesn't make this thing a cow. The guy inside must've been sprayed with some kind of specially made 'stockyard perfume.' But—wait. 'Cowman' just stuck out his tongue at me. And it's a foot long tongue! Like a real cow! No, his tongue must be fake too. Or he's all fake—and is a hologram? Or maybe that pill I paid my lawyer to hide in my shoe…it's giving me hallucinations? Or, or, is-is-is the federal government doing all this to make me think I'm crazy—or to drive me crazy? Or am I…"

"No. You're not dreaming, Ronald," Cowman's deep voice finished Scott's thoughts. "I am a cow and a lawyer, and you're on trial for mass murder."

"But—I was just an actor; reading off of cue cards! I didn't kill anyone! Sam Jefferson is responsible for those 39 people."

"Who cares about those 39 stupid nutrition challenged humans? This trial is about you taking part in mass murdering billions of cows."

"What?!"

Cowlawyer stepped to the side to show Scott that he was in a courtroom, and that the spectators, the jury, the judge, the lawyers and the bailiff were all cows wearing "human clothes." A Bible was placed in front of Scott's right hand and Cowbailiff asked:

"Do you swear to tell the whole truth and nothing but the truth, so help you God?"

Scott felt that if he was going to be tried as Donald McRonald by cows, then he'd no longer be Scott Willard. He'd be his alter-ego, and Donald McRonald is damn proud to represent the greatest company in the world; he isn't about to let a dumb, smelly Cowlawyer embarrass him.

"You bet your burgers I do!" Scott answered in his raspy Donald McRonald voice. "Speaking of burgers, is this the Nurem-burger trial, cow counsel?"

"We call it justice," Cowlawyer said.

"And we call Donald McRonald its minister of propaganda!" a Cowspectator yelled.

"Order in the court!" Cowjudge said as he slammed his gavel. "Proceed, counsel."

"Mr. McRonald. Is it true that you and your superiors are responsible for the mass murder of billions of cows?"

"I was never made aware of that number."

"You represent a gazillion dollar corporation, but don't know how it earns its assets?" he scoffed.

"My leaders only told me what they wanted me to know," Scott answered, looking into Cowlawyer's huge brown eyes.

"Which was…?"

"Two all-beef patties, signature sauce, lettuce, cheese, tomatoes, onions on a sesame bun. You read me?"

"No, but you are a well-read clown, are you not?"

"You're talking to a valedictorian of Hamburger State University."

"And as such, you're required to attend many a McRonald's store opening, yes?"

"If I didn't, I'd be terminated—in more than one way."

Cowlawyer opened a legal folder and removed an 8½ " x 11" photograph of two yellow arches standing in a typical McRonald's parking lot. Three other stuffed folders were marked "Exhibit A – Apple Pie," "Exhibit B – Big Mack," and "Exhibit C - Cheeseburger."

"Let it be known to this court that at the time of Mr. McRonald's arrest, this learned clown could not read his flagship store's two story sign proclaiming, '100 billion served.'"

"That sign is wrong!"

"So it's not 100 billion 'terminated?'"

"We hit the hundred billion mark in 1999. I'm proud to say that the death toll and our profit margin changes every second."

"Then to your knowledge, what is the current number?"

"Actually—my records were lost in the last burger war."

Cowlawyer reached into another legal folder and removed a photograph of another McRonald's sign showing:

"As of this very date, 999 billion bovines have lost their lives! Is this sign correct? Or do all your yellow arches lie like you about the heifer holocaust?"

"No, they and I never lie. But, can we call a recess? I feel a 'Big Mack Assault' coming on."

"There was a good reason why your company used the word 'assault' in that ad campaign. For that's what you did to innocent cows—like this one!"

Cowlawyer placed his hands under his bench, and emerged holding a Big Mack. Every cow in the courtroom gasped and cried, knowing that the Big Mack might very well be the remains of a loved one. Cowlawyer waved it before Donald's face.

"You used my kind to quench your thirst for watered down blood, didn't you? How many innocent creatures will you put in slaughter houses before the world screams, 'Enough!' How many Styrofoam, quarter-pound caskets will pollute this planet for eternity? How many acres of land will this company devour and waste for profit? How many arteries will you permanently clog? Mr. McRonald, have you no shame?"

"I was only following orders."

"And whose may those be? We want names, Mr. McRonald. Who was your superior?"

"It was—the Grimmice!"

"Do you expect this court to believe some mumbling, Muppet-headed goofball named 'Grimmice,' the twenty year old simpleton stepson of Sam Jefferson, he's the mastermind behind a mass genocide?!"

"He was! Grimmice was the one who wanted to conquer the world. He-he—he said domination in America wasn't enough. No, Grimmice wanted Europe in the palms of his white gloved hands. He took over Poland, then Czechoslovakia then...then…he wanted to digest it all -with a large Coca Cola! And—he wanted to terminate me because he's thirty years younger than I am and wants my job!"

"That is not true and you know it. We are waiting."

As Cowattorney looked away for a split second, Ronald grabbed "Exhibit A – Apple Pie," and held it like it was a knife.

"You'll never take me alive!"

"Look out! He's holding a hot apple pie!" a Cowspecatator shouted.

"And I know how to use it! Now back off. Or—or--"

"You'll what? He's speechless! He can't say anything unless someone tells him what to say!"

"I'll burn my brains out!"

"If you think that'll make this world a better place: burn, clownie, burn."

Scott bit into the apple pie, swallowed and felt as if every organ in his body was on fire. He doubled over in the chair, which only caused a chorus of laughter to ring throughout the courtroom. Scott tried to stand only to fall to his knees and beg for help. Mocking voices replied:

"Ha! We should help you?"

"Listen to Donald! A mass murderer is asking his victims to help?"

"How did you help us?"

"I'll help you when you help me find my family you slaughtered!"

"Make us all happy and croak, Donny!"

"Die, Donald, die!" a voice yelled. Immediately, everyone in the courtroom, including the judge, chanted for the end of Donald McRonald's reign of terror.

"Die, Donald, die! Die, Donald, die! Die, Donald, die! Die, Donald, die! DIE!"

Scott weakly saluted and whispered, "Long live McRonald Land!"

****

Scott heard Cowlawyer say, "He's coming to." Scott was afraid to open his eyes. When he did, he saw not a roomful of cows, but one human; a human doctor standing beside his bed.

"Where am I?" Scott asked.

"You've been in a three-day coma. Now you're in Tampa General Hospital."

"For what? Trying to kill myself in prison?"

"Is 'prison' opening up a McRonald's in Hornet's Nest, Florida in 110 degree weather?"

"No, that's not prison. That's real fun but—wait a minute. You said I was in a coma?"

"For three days and counting. A combination of heat exhaustion and a heart attack has been known to do that."

"So I've never been in prison? Or in a courtroom for, for mass murder? And there was no McRonald's E-coli outbreak?"

"Not that I know of. But the day is young. Man, you must've had one crazy dream. That's all." They turned their attention to the nightstand's ringing phone. Scott answered it and was delighted to hear Sam Jefferson's voice.

"How are you doing, kid?"

"Great. Never felt better in my life!" Scott said as his doctor left the room.

"You're a good liar, Scott. Um, Scott. I've always looked at you as a second son to me who, who knows w-w-when—"

"Hold on. Whenever you stammer, I know something's eating at you."

"Yeah. This is hard for me to do because I look at you as a second son to me, but…I'm afraid I have to let you go."

"You mean—as in fire me?"

"Yes. McRonald's can't have an unhealthy Donald McRonald. I mean, there you were; one minute, you're opening up a store, the next minute, you're being shoved into an ambulance in your Donald McRonald costume. And here we are, trying to pitch our product as good, healthy food that's good for you, and there you are, looking like death. And death is not good P.R. Are you still there, Scott?"

Scott wiped a tear from his face and said, "Physically, I'm still here. Mentally…is it my age, Sam? Is that it? I'm too old to play the part?"

"Not at all. People get exhausted by heat and get heart attacks at any age."

"Then, who could replace me?"

"'The Grimmice.' You know, huh, my stepson, Joey."

"You mean your twenty year old stepson. A twenty year old who trumps my age by 38."

"Again, it's not his age, Scott. He's only moving up in the ranks."

"Yahvole, mien commadent," Scott said in an exaggerated German accent.

"And yahvole to you, Donald. Time to hand in your size 45 shoes," Sam snarled, hanging up the phone.

Scott stared at the ceiling, sobbed and sang a version of his national anthem:

"I deserve a break today, so get up and get away, to McRonald's!"

Diary of a Dead Man

by Ashton Macauly

It started simply with two individuals sitting in a coffee shop. One was Brian, a young, not-all-too-handsome man, with a slender frame. The other was a woman, dark, also slender, but with a shrewd look about her. Brian gazed down at the freshly wiped glass of the table as his coffee cup leaked new stains onto its surface.

"Come on; tell me what you've got. It's been months and you haven't shown me a single page."

"I'm nervous," said Brian, taking a diplomatic sip from his coffee. "This could be it; this could be the one that finally takes me out of this shithole. No offense." The woman moved her arms in a placating gesture.

"None taken. It's rough out here, I know. I used to be here, and I'm doing my best to help take you out, but you've got to give me something to go on."

"Alright, here goes." Brian cleared his throat. "*I look into the mirror with tired eyes, soft, bleary, and full of regret. The years have been kind to me and yet I have not. I have no right to feel this way. The world was handed to me on a silver platter, but still I stand, watching myself decay, slowly, but surely passing into the abyss. How many days more will I stand here? 5,000? Or 5? It haunts me to know that the years of my youth are now passed and I stand on the threshold of making a new life. One step out of the door lies disgrace, or greatness. If only I had the wanderer's feet to move."*

They sat in silence, sipping their coffees. She stroked her long brown hair, staring out the window for a moment at the stream of cars racing by. Brian could not tell if she was impressed, bewildered, or perhaps both. For the most part, he had worried that his writing would come off as a bit too depressing. "Come on Shannon, give it to me straight. Is it any good?"

"It's morbid, for sure, but I think you're on to something. I want the first ten pages in my inbox this afternoon. None of that waiting three days shit. I think I've got a whole load of middle-aged mothers just unsatisfied enough to read it." She reached for her wallet.

"No, please, let me," he said in an attempt to be polite. In reality, the coffees would have just about broken his nearly empty wallet.

"Hey, you might be a big shot soon. Then you can buy the coffees." She left ten dollars on the table and started to leave. "Listen. If any of that's real, you might want to see someone. I can't be losing my clients to 'emotional outbursts', if you catch my drift." It was all too well known in her industry that writers have a tendency to overindulge in spirits and cozy up to the deceptive friendship offered by the barrel of a shotgun.

"No problem! I'll e-mail it to you right now." He looked genuinely excited. Someone liked his work; it was the beginning of a new life for him. People were going to notice him and hear his words. He hopped up from the table and bounded into the street, where he was promptly obliterated by a semi-truck.

A Scientific Martyr

Years later, Brian stood at the back of a crowded auditorium, watching in silence as Dr. Coulton's prominent scientific career ground to a halt.

The white haired man standing behind the pulpit had no idea how close he was to committing academic suicide. "I have dedicated my life's work to the field of quantum mechanics, but tonight I want to talk to you about something of a more fantastic nature. For eons, the human race has wondered what happens after death. Our final journey is both a mysterious and terrifying one."

"What if death is not the end? What if there is a world beyond this one where we can live on if we so choose? Where ghosts are no longer a thing of mythology and fear, but rather a reality, and one that we must learn to accept, study, and live in peace with. Poltergeists and possessions should not be topics of fear, but of debate and scientific inquiry."

The shocked looks of the academics in the audience brought a grimace to Brian's face. The dark corner cast a sinister shadow over him, but he could not risk sitting out in the open. His attire was not suitable for a symposium. Holes and dirt adorned his long-faded jeans, and while his jacket may have at one point been fashionable, it was now torn and frayed beyond recognition. He shouldn't have been in the theatre at all, but he had waited for this speech for a long time.

Brian fumed. Why couldn't the community see how close to the truth Dr. Coulton's theory was? Like many great minds before him, Coulton's ideas were not met with applause, but with pitchforks. Brian scanned the audience. A few of them were still paying attention, but most looked as though they were sharpening their criticisms in the dark. Dr. Coulton was sweating profusely and fumbling with his notecards. His glorious opening was meant to be met with awe and wonderment, and instead there was only muted sniggering from the back rows.

"As we are all no doubt aware, the effects of quantum observers have long been debated. Can the mere act of observing an object or action change the outcome or meaning of said action? More simply: Does standing next to a falling tree affect the sound it makes? Through my research, I have come to believe that the world of the recently deceased operates on a similar principle." Several of the chief university funders walked out of the lecture hall shaking their heads; Dr. Coulton was determined to continue.

"The existence of ghosts or specters is only possible through our own enabling. The mythos and energy we have created around death allows us to continue on afterward." That was the turning point where Nobel Prize laureate Alex Coulton took a risk and found himself cast out. Ideas that may have seemed profound at the time of their conception, instead turned into tick marks on a pink slip.

He made it on stage for a full twenty minutes before the crowd began to boo. Brian was the only one who kept his eyes on Dr. Coulton the whole time, but unfortunately, the opinions of the deceased don't count for much. In the end, the crowd erupted into a tempest of criticism, and Brian could no longer bear to watch. *Maybe the next one will get it right.* Everyone was so busy shouting and throwing bits of paper that none of them noticed the temporal disturbance at the back of the theatre as Brian faded from view, the theatre disappearing as he stepped back into the world between worlds.

On the Subject of Being Dead

Brian was 21 years dead, still the spitting image of his late twenties (aside from the road rash, a lingering reminder of his unfortunate little accident) and sported unkempt, black hair that hung just above his eyes. He stepped out of that lecture hall feeling a sense of despair. One of the last hopes for the field of paranormal science had fallen, and would likely soon join the ranks of the recently deceased (halting careers have a tendency to do that to people.) Unfortunately for Dr. Coulton, the scientific witch hunt that ensued would follow him for the rest of his short life.

Tiny white lights popped into existence around Brian as he faded from the lecture hall. They were the souls of those who had recently passed on being ferried through the cosmic goop that bound the two worlds together. Ordinarily, Brian wouldn't have bothered with the trip (something about the goo made him uncomfortable), but it was far faster when traveling long distances. It was only a matter of minutes from the time he left the lecture hall in New Hampshire to when he popped into the dingy interior of one of the oldest hotels in New Orleans.

The Hotel Chambroux was built in the late 1800s to accommodate a sudden population boom, but hadn't really changed with the times. Its hallways were filled with an unsettling, musty smell, peeling yellow paint, and more spirits than could be counted in a lifetime. Most of the hotel's visitors came for the sordid history and a chance at seeing some ghosts from the era of its inception. For the most part this endeavor was futile, as most of the older ghosts had gone and moved on. Limbo can entertain the dead for a while, but sooner or later everyone has to leave.

Brian let out a heavy sigh; more of a ghostly wisp, really, but it's going through the motions that counts. With death came an awful amount of sadness. The only way to keep it at bay was to engage in a constant stream of distractions. The lecture had ended, and there was still five hours before Brian's next shift. For that time, it was just him and his thoughts. The poor boy had been sandwiched between a semi-truck and a telephone pole, and always had a hard time moving on from it.

In a fortuitous turn of events, a psychologist had taken his own life four months earlier in one of the hotel bathtubs, and took up residence in the crawlspace between the twelfth and fourteenth floors (superstition leaves a lot of open real estate for the deceased). Brian had only visited twice, and as a result had started journaling. It was depressing drivel for the most part, but it seemed to make things a little less miserable. In fact, the thought of writing a few more lines of meaningless bullshit on that ethereal paper was the only thing propelling Brian forward.

He shivered as he passed through a business man and what had to be a cheap hooker. The world of the living and the world of the dead exist almost in parallel. There are some small differences to be sure, but for the most part they are identical. As a member of the deceased, Brian was able to see both of these worlds at once, which led to a rather comical ballet of the dead and the living passing right through each other as they went about their daily business.

The crap that the History Channel spouts about chills being associated with the dead couldn't be farther from the truth. If it were true, the Hotel Chambroux would have more closely resembled an ice box, instead of the less-than-desirable temporary accommodation it was. As a general rule, the dead never outnumber the living, but certain spaces are more heavily populated than others. The top three locations for the dead to inhabit are Cemeteries, Old Hotels, and places of religious worship. Beliefs about life after death keep the morbid image and mythos of death alive, meaning more space for lost souls.

Brian had dedicated his afterlife to keeping that image alive. Most of the recently deceased are met with two options if they wish to keep on existing: strike out on their own and try to haunt one person (always a gamble), or join up with a large group (like a hotel) and work as a team. Most opted for the second option, but a few notable ghosts have made it on the first (looking at you Bloody Mary).

New Orleans was the perfect town for Brian to land in. It had one of the highest beliefs in voodoo in the United States, cemeteries on every corner, and enough ghost stories to maintain millions of the recently deceased. This highly susceptible population is what allowed Brian to stick around and sulk in the unfinished business that he thought was so important. He used to say he stayed to try and sort out the whirlwind of emotion that had come on the heels of his death, but mostly he just liked to scare the shit out of people.

Worked to Death

After hours of sulking and writing snide comments in his journal, Brian walked into a crowded staffroom. What appeared as an aging utility closet to mortals was actually a place of meeting and organized chaos to the undead. Standing at the front of the room was a tall, skinny, Frenchman who had suffered cirrhosis of the liver at 45 after his wife had left him for a German body builder. In haphazard rows sat the inhabitants of the hotel, impatient as ever. Attire was a mix of the old and the new, with modern styles only recently beginning to surface. It was an unfortunate side effect of everyone being stuck in the clothes that they had died in.

"Alright, welcome everyone," said the Frenchman at the front of the room. Keeping ghosts in one place and attentive was a difficult task, and one that only Jacque was able to manage. "The holiday season is coming up, so we really need to be on our game." He was referring to October, the one month out of the year where for no apparent reason, the human population seemed to take leave of their senses. Those on earth abandoned the principles of hard logic and scientific discipline in search of the unknown, and ghosts loved to exploit it. More than half the hotel's hauntings occurred in October, and it was those ghost stories that kept them in business the rest of the year.

"Today is a busy day. I've got a group of Atheists on the 3rd floor that look like they might be about to make the jump into skepticism. Molly, Shannon, I need you to do a grieving woman and a creepy twin at midnight and 2AM. I want them screaming at the top of their lungs and clutching at their shorts when they leave the building." Atheists were one of the toughest groups to deal with, but for the undead, screwing with someone's world views, while difficult, was very rewarding.

"Edward!" A man in a powdered wig and a civil war uniform stood up straight and saluted. The man had never even been in the army, but when alive, had participated in Sunday war reenactments, where he had died from a stray lawn dart. Most thought he had it coming, as he always fought for The South. "You're going to be the ghost of General Pillam. There's a group from the history channel trying to summon him on the twelfth floor. They should be holding a séance around 3:15AM."

"Yes, sir, I'll be there, sir." Edward straightened his doublet and sat back down, one of the few dead who remained at attention.

"Fantastic. Brian, Megan, you're on poltergeist duty. There's a writer on floor 12 and a couple that think it's a good idea to hide away in the ballroom for a quickie. Show them the error of their ways, and make a real mess of it. That ballroom used to be one of my favorite parts of this hotel."

"Christ," Poltergeist duty was the lowest of the low. No one liked to do it. The ghosts in charge never got to show their faces, and as a result didn't get much credit for it. Throwing books and lamps around a room was only entertaining for so long.

"What was that?" asked the Frenchman with an indignant stare.

A young woman named Megan piped up from beside Brian. "Nothing, we'll be there." She was cute for a manic depressive. The scars on her arms didn't even obscure her beauty all that much.

If I had a sex drive, thought Brian. An unfortunate side effect of rigor mortis and trans-dimensional relocation was a complete loss of sexual appetite. "Yes, we'll be there," said Brian with a reluctant shrug. He didn't have much of a choice in the matter. If he disobeyed the order, he would likely be on the street the next day. Ghosts are a crotchety bunch, and don't tolerate failure.

"Good. Everyone else, you're on thermostats, disembodied footsteps and mournful wailing. Make it cold, and make it creepy!" Most ghosts don't make it to the big show. They end up performing minor acts that cause discomfort and anxiety for the hotel patrons. It's surprising how little it takes for a room to get a reputation as haunted. They're right, of course, but still, there isn't much for them to go on.

The meeting concluded and Brian and Megan stepped out into one of the hotel's many aging hallways. Bellhops were crisscrossing the floor like madmen as guests poured in for the holiday season. The hotel would be full in a day or so, which meant more work for all of its employees, both living and dead. Business kept Brian's mind busy, which he liked, as it kept him away from his own darker corners.

"You've got to stop mouthing off to him," Megan was fond of lecturing Brian after every misstep he made. Brian was fond of making missteps just to watch the wheels turn.

"I hardly think that an exasperated sigh counts as mouthing off," he said with a sigh equally as exasperated as the first. Megan gave him a look that only those who are dead are capable of mustering.

"Just because we're dead doesn't mean you have to be miserable about it. We've got things pretty good here."

"I'm not miserable. I'm just unsatisfied."

"Well if you'd rather take the express train down below and shack up with a demon, no one is stopping you."

"What makes you so sure I'm going down?"

"Most of us wouldn't be here if we weren't. We've received an extension; a time to come to peace with our demons before we have to actually face them."

"You don't believe in second chances?"
.
"No. If we were going to go to heaven, we'd be there. Nothing we do here is worthy of clemency."

"We do a good thing."

She gave him the look again. "Terrifying nuns and small children as if they are the devil himself is a good thing? I think you've got the fairy tales backwards."

"We give people the time to deal with unfinished business. Without it, what else would there be?" They stopped in front of a door with the number 1242 on it.

"You're fooling yourself. What do you want to be this time: Books or faucets and alarm clocks?" Most people wouldn't have even bothered to ask.

"Books," he said, still managing to maintain his overdramatic and melancholy air.

"Alright, let's get to work."

The Working Stiff

"So you didn't get your fair shake at life; that's no reason to go around moping about it. Throw yourself into your work; do something with what you've got."

"Look, I don't exactly think now is the best time to be discussing this. Can you hit the alarm?" Megan bashed the bedside table and the clock alarm began to sound. The room was dimly lit, giving it an eerie vibe. Dim lighting was always an advantage for the dead; it would cast shadows that they could take credit for. Crossing over into the physical plane was not an easy feat, and even then could only be sustained briefly. For that reason, hauntings usually occurred at night and in places not often serviced by competent electricians.

In the corner of the room was the writer. He was a short man, hunched over the desk, and scribbling furiously on a yellow legal pad lit only by the desk lamp. The rest of the room was shrouded in darkness. When the alarm went off, he barely paid it any head and continued to jot down whatever seemed so important to him. "Typical.

Supernatural events going on right behind him and he's so absorbed in his work that he can't even take a moment to notice."

Brian picked up a book from one of the decorative shelves adorning the room and tossed it at the bedside. The mirror next to it would have made a fine demonstration of force, but too much damage would have meant the room shutting down for maintenance. Fewer rooms meant fewer patrons, which in turn meant less potential for haunting. Brian would always make a mess, but never so much as to overly inconvenience the hotel staff. After all, it was his business as much as it was theirs.

The writer turned briefly at the noise from the book, revealing an ugly, but recognizable face in the shadowy light. "Holy shit! I know him!" exclaimed Brian. The mundane world of his daily work had quickly become one of the most exciting moments of his life, and afterlife for that matter. He felt as though blood pumped through his veins, even though there was nothing but ethereal dust holding him together.

"What? Is he your old boss or something?" Brian let his jaw hang open, shocked by Megan's lack of knowledge.

"No, that's J.P. Morowitz."

"Who?"

"The famous author? Seventeen Seconds to Midnight?"

"Never heard of him."

"Did you even read?" The lack of literary depth in the spirit form that was Megan appalled Brian in a most visceral sense. He felt as though he was going to be sick, even though once again it would have been wholly impossible.

"Dickens, Vonnegut, Voltaire; yes I read, but nothing by this man. Now get off your pedestal, stop being star struck and let's get back to business." Brian had stopped paying attention and was already walking over to the table, curious as to what the great writer was working on. "Damn it, Brian. You know what happens if we're late, right? Is this really worth it?"

Brian continued to ignore her, reading over the man's hunched shoulder. "This isn't a new novel," An air of melancholy overtook Brian's usually sarcastic presence. "It's a suicide note." His heart sunk. People had told him that good artists were always tortured in some way, but he had never really believed it. The mediocrity that had been his life had fueled hundreds of unread books, and he hadn't thought even once about taking his own life. In a way, it explained why none of them had ever been read.

"Look on the bright side. Maybe you'll get to meet your hero after all," Megan displayed a grin that was far too jovial for the situation.

"This isn't funny."

"Sorry." She rolled her eyes a full three-hundred-and-sixty degrees (another perk of the undead). "When did you become so sensitive?"

Brian brushed off her rebuke. It was a moment of realization for him, and he was desperate to hold on to it. "I don't get it. He's at the top of his career, he's never written a bad book, and he has a loving family waiting for him at home. He's going to throw all that away in a dingy hotel room?"

"Sounds like the perfect addition to our staff." Megan continued to mock his concern. Brian threw books as hard as he could, tipping over furniture, and breaking whatever he could get his hands on. Moving objects wasn't easy, but he was in a rage. He couldn't comprehend the fundamental selfishness that his childhood hero was displaying. The man had everything that Brian had ever wanted in life, and was prepared to throw it all away.

The poltergeist on display was one of the most magnificent that the hotel had ever seen. If there had been a dead musician on staff, there was no doubt that he would have written symphonies in its honor. Books floated in perfect, unnerving unison, the alarm clocks all went off at once, and the lights even flickered in time with the ghostly wails of the workers on the floor above. It was straight out of a Hitchcock movie, and at the end of it, the result was the same.

"Well if he wasn't going to kill himself, he sure is now."
Megan had seen Brian fly off the handle before, and didn't
want to waste the effort to try and calm him.

"Oh God, no," said Brian, his voice dropping to a whisper.
J.P. stood on a chair that had been hastily stood upright in
the calamity, and fastened a leather belt to the sturdy-
looking ceiling fan at the center of the room. He wore a
look of grim determination. "Stop," yelled Brian,
transcending briefly into physical form. The sight must have
been truly terrifying, as the shock was enough to startle J.P.
and send him tumbling off of his chair. There was a sharp
snap, and Brian watched as the author whom he had
admired all throughout life died.

What Not to Do

Highest on the list of things ghosts shouldn't do is
terminally interacting with the living (it is in bold, large
print, and listed twice). It's somewhere between setting a
blimp ablaze with supernatural fire because a long lost wife
was on it with her new husband (that's right, the dead
ruined the zeppelin industry for everyone,) and popping out
of a jack in the box as a gruesome, but personable severed
head at a child's birthday party (not as bad, but equally
terrifying). When Brian watched J.P. swing from the rope,
he had two emotions: 1. Jaw-dropping, pants-shitting fear
regarding the omnipotent repercussions that were no doubt
on their way, and 2. Profound sadness at the thankless
nature of his childhood hero's life. It was the second that
held his attention.

"You killed him," said Megan, providing a realistic backdrop for what had become insanity.

"You act like it's a terrible thing. You're dead; I'm dead; what's another to the pile?"

"You killed him!"

"Not on purpose." Again, he tried to minimalize the situation. The truth was still bobbing on the surface of his mind, failing to sink in. The standard protocol for breaches like the one he had just committed was swift and brutal. He would be called in for questioning, taken by requisition agents (a rather pompous group of imbeciles who do the work of Death,) judged by a group of unsatisfied ex-despots, and subsequently thrown onto an express train to the underworld. Things couldn't have been much worse for him.

"Do you even understand what you've just done?" Megan was speaking in a terse whisper.

Brian stood remarkably still under the swinging corpse, lost in thought. *He had it all; the dream, the talent; everything. He had it in his palm and he threw it away.* Brian's thoughts drifted to what might have been had he heeded traffic on that warm summer afternoon. Maybe his book would have been published, and maybe he could have been as great as J.P. The scenario played like an old film clip in his head: first there was the money, then the drugs, the fame, and finally the end of a rope, where he too swung, awaiting a man in a grey suit to ferry him along to the next place. "It wouldn't have mattered at all."

"Of course it matters. You just killed a man, Brian. They're going to come for you any minute now. In fact, I'm surprised they're not already here." Brian's arms and legs began to tingle with an unfamiliar sensation. He no longer wanted to return to the land of living, and his life was but a distant memory. The realization of how it could have ended made the thought of living even an instant longer nauseating. He looked down at his hands as they began to fade from existence.

"Megan."

"Do something. Run. Anything."

"It doesn't matter anymore," He held up his hands to explain. The world lost focus around him. The drab walls of the hotel peeled and gave way to pillars of silver and gold. Megan still stood before him, but soon faded as well. "It's better than you could have ever imagined." In reality, it felt a bit like being stuffed in an oversized pillow, but Brian wanted to leave the end shrouded in a positive mystery for the moment when Megan finally crossed over herself.

Megan mouthed words at him, but they fell on deaf ears. Brian was being dragged upward with vicious force. Clouds flew by on both sides, and in the swirling anarchy he thought that he glimpsed other souls, passing too quickly to be seen in detail. This continued for twenty seconds, and then reality slammed into him with alarming force. He was standing in the middle of an old hotel room, arms outstretched to imaginary heavens, and an idiotic look of rapturous content spread across his face.

"You're going to be dragged to hell Brian."

"Oh shit."

"Yes oh shit. Run!" On deadened legs he half ran, half glided through the hotel walls, passing secret moments and furtive glances hidden behind locked doors. Failing marriages and family vacations flew by at a blinding pace. He had just passed through a room where a principle sat cross-legged on the floor contemplating his life choices when he came to the end of a long hallway.

"Don't move." The voice resonated through the air, cold as ice, and fast as a bullet. A man in a bloody black suit stood at the end with a veritable hand cannon raised and pointed at Brian's head. "Times up, let's not make a mess." In a moment of panic and unfathomable stupidity, Brian turned and ran. Behind him there was a loud bang, and his leg dropped out from under him. Ethereal dust blew away from the wound and into the air conditioning vents. He fell to his remaining knee, and watched helplessly as the man sidled up to him.

"You're lucky. That'll grow back." The recently dead had an easier time regenerating than those who had been decomposing for some time. The man extended his hand, and with great reluctance, Brian took it.

"So this is it then? Headed on to the express train down."

"That's not for me to decide." The room disappeared in a flash of white.

Judge, Jury, and...

When the white light evaporated, Brian was standing in front of four men. They were dressed in military outfits and sat at the top of a large wooden bench. Brian was in the court of appeals, a place dedicated to listening to sob stories of redemption, and then rejecting them. Rejection involved a large metal lever that had been painted a friendly red color. When pulled, it released the floorboards beneath the defendant and they fell straight down to hell. The tribunal was made up of warlords who felt they hadn't had their fair shake at world domination. This made them a cantankerous bunch, and more often than not 'trigger happy'.

"Welcome, Brian, to the high court of the fallen," said a man clad in military garb with a deep African accent. The four men looked down on him with contemptuous stares. He felt as though he was sweating, even though his pores no longer existed.

"Look, it was a complete accident. I didn't mean to,"

"We don't really have time for this; your sentencing is mostly a formality." The man speaking was a civil war general who still sported a white handlebar mustache and a uniform with a confederate flag on it. His southern drawl was terrifying in a way it had no right to be. Brian quaked on the marble floor below.

"I understand," said Brian, his head falling low with apprehension. Back on Earth, Brian had pictured Hell often, but for the most part with the satirical lens of a cynic (or a writer). In those days, it had never been real, but as he stood on the cusp of its fiery gates, he felt the gravity of it sinking in. Somewhere below his feet awaited an infinite array of torture, decay, and malice.

"Your request to pass on has been approved. Next." The civil war general was already shredding the paperwork pertaining to Brian's case.

"Wait, what?" Before he was able to get a response, Brian was ushered out of the marble room by a pair of strong hands. He was dragged into a long, gold corridor. At the end was a man, sitting at a brown desk, shuffling through stacks of paper that stretched up to the top of the far-too-high ceiling.

"Ah, Brian is it?" The man's voice was high and nasally.

"Yes. What did they mean--"

"I'm sorry to cut you off, but tight schedule and all. Here are your wings, halo, and journal."

"I'm sorry?" Brian said, and in a sudden moment of immense pain, wings shot from his shoulder blades and a halo burned into existence above his head.

"Oh the journal? We've found that eternal pleasure can actually be rather dull sometimes. The Big Man thought it might help for you to write about it. You are a writer, correct?"

"Yes, but—"

"Splendid, off you go then." From beneath his feat a trap door opened revealing a set of heavy metal coils. Without warning, they sprung up and launched him into the air. White clouds, salmon haze, and a series of violet streaks turned around him in a terrible rhythm. *Heaven could really use a few interior decorators*, was all he thought before he passed out.

When he awoke, Brian was in a small room. It was very similar to the apartment he had inhabited in the months before his demise. On a white coffee table, there was a short note. *Congratulations Brian, you did it. We were all rooting for you. —God.* Initially, the note from the creator shocked and humbled Brian, but soon after found out it was merely a formality composed by a persnickety choir of angels. The fact of the matter was God was busy (crashing planes in the Bermuda Triangle to be precise).

For a while, Brian thought not of the circumstances surrounding his judgement for fear of reprisal. After several months, however, curiosity got the better of him. One day after the hundredth or so round of shuffleboard with Mahatma Gandhi, Brian asked the unthinkable. "Why didn't I get sent to hell?" For a moment the question lingered in the air, and then Gandhi began to laugh.

"Divine intervention." He continued to laugh and reset the board for another game. "It's like God's way of saying, sorry for the truck."

Brian took a minute to process, but realized that either way it was over and done with. "He could have just sent flowers." With that they both started laughing and Brian began to feel at ease with the injustice surrounding his death. They continued their game as the artificial sun above set over the endless stretches of heavenly clouds.

As time passed, even all the pleasures that his heart could desire weren't enough to satisfy Brian. He returned to the passion that had once driven him in life. The rest of his eternity was spent writing dull poetry about the color white and angel wings, but he was happy.

Summer in Seattle

By M.T. Roberts

Lincoln Meab walked like a man reneged of interest in the world, and despite the loud, pulsing claps from his cane, he went unnoticed among the afternoon's mass of city goers, moving brisk in his brown suit between the shadows of Seattle in 1993.

He disliked the city. To him, there was a stench that permeated and throbbed beyond any olfactory, as if there were a pool of worn-out bile kept hidden beneath the streets and avenues, now getting run over in late traffic; and he knew their names, those streets and avenues. At this time of year, steam fumed from the man-holes, he imagined the steam was a less staunch version of what really bubbled beyond their covers just below, in the sewer.

He smelled meat and piss and that crystalline graze of
Autumn-feel which haunts the air when October is near.

Lincoln Meab twitched a frown and cornered off First
Avenue, heading up the way of South Washington Street.
There was a park, he remembered, past the next block; there
would be so many things to see for a man like him—so
many people.

He took a seat on a wooden bench and bent his knees,
wincing, drawing in his feet and soundly listening to his old
shoes as they dragged over dead leaves and cold cement.
His leather satchel lay next to him; it looked plump from the
things he brought stuffed inside. Lincoln Meab watched
over it for several minutes, pleased and calm, observing the
tiny spider cracks and dark tans on its surface. He alternated
from his satchel to the hobos to the office girls passing by in
the city park.

He got the tinge of excitement he always relished when dreaming this scene at home in his basement, but living in the moment, it soared across his chest, writhing and popping. He kept still, and told himself he would have to do this with care. Lincoln Meab reached into his bloated, worn satchel, digging around another object bigger than the one he wanted, his gloved hands almost a hindrance. *Oh, they're gonna like this*, he thought, *these are special…*

Pigeons came and cooed little twirps around his ankles. He scattered small white pieces in his palm and let his mouth part, noticing his breath in the chill air. The sun was drowning, he liked to think, and on Fall days like this, it was laziness if one did not observe its bleak beauty among the trees through the high buildings. Even down to the paper and trash that billowed over the park's floor, the sun's tired glow impressed its own weariness on everything it touched.

The day grew lower.

Lincoln Meab withdrew from his pleasure of looking, feeling as though these moments would be well recalled with fondness, and reached back into his satchel, freeing the bigger item kept there. Placing it behind him, he rose slow and steadied his cane, hooking the strap of his satchel over a slouched shoulder. With one last intake of the park, he moved, tipping the wide brim of his hat down against the cooling breeze.

A man and his dog walked toward the bench about half an hour later. The man's dog stopped in front of it, smelling the ghosted pigeons and lapping at something tiny and white. The man was hurried and tugged at his poodle with the leash. "C'mon," he said, "Hey, leave it!"

He pulled his dog away and stepped closer to see what it was scouring. The street lights flickered on, casting a dull yellow hue over the bench. The man's eyes adjusted and he reeled back, seeing a small tooth.

Without thinking, he began to leave. "C'mon, let's go," he said, but continued to stare, distracted. As he slowed away from the bench he noticed more scattered teeth, some crushed into powder from the shoes of others. When he saw a long sandwich wrapped in tin foil on the bench, he dismissed the teeth and went home, walking up to Second and ready to guard against the homeless.

By the time Lincoln Meab reached his house in northern Queen Anne, the temperature had dropped well into the forties. He fumbled with his lock and reached inside to flip on the porch lights, looking into his mail box on the outer wall. His heart pumped. There was a letter. He came inside and closed the door, taking his time toward the kitchen, where he turned on the inside lights. He hung his coat and poured a glass of gin, sitting down crooked at the table. He opened the letter and paused.

Mr. Meab, I am sending you another package. You will receive it tomorrow morning prompt at 7:28. Please adhere

its contents to section A7 and return your pictures per
usual.
-Grey Irion

Lincoln Meab groaned like a puppy and looked up to his owl clock on the kitchen wall. He moved into the living room and put the letter in his fireplace. It was cold inside the house, but he refrained from starting a fire. Maybe he would stop burning the letters, too. He thought about making an egg, but decided he should get to work cleaning up downstairs; removing section A7 earlier that morning had been messier than he thought. He grabbed the bottle of gin and went to his hallway, unlocking the basement door. Fumes wafted up, disturbing his eyes like always.

*   *   *   *

"Coke?"
Summer came into work from lunch and saw her cubicle still mussed from earlier.
"No thanks," she replied.

Jeremy, an intern who ate at his desk, shrugged and turned around to dip down into his own cubicle.

"But if you change your mind," he said, un-seeable now, "it'll cost you."

"Is that so? Well, I'm glad I prefer Pepsi then."

Jeremy laughed.

"Did you read the paper?" he asked.

"No, I've been busy," Summer said flipping her rolodex, trying to correlate a client's name with another client's number while putting her purse away for the afternoon stint.

"Well, second page," he said, "There's this story about a kid's arm being found on a bench in Pioneer Square."

"Really?"

"Yeah, city cleaner found it late last night, it was wrapped in tin foil—"

"Oh my god, that's awful! Do they know who did it?"

"Nope, not yet."

She splayed her hands, disgusted, casting big shadows over her work.

"But yeah," Jeremy continued, "I guess they found some teeth in the area too, and from what I read, the police think they might be the same—"

"Jeremy, I need to finish this before two…"

"Okay, okay. Sorry, sorry."

She heard him begin to type on his calculator.

"Summer?"

She flicked her pen to her desk, annoyed.

"Yeah?"

"That coke'll still cost you."

She let out a stressed laugh.

After work, Summer was out on the street, and the Fourth Avenue traffic seemed like it might get uglier than the weather—which, Summer thought, was saying a lot. Had she felt normal, she might have splurged and taken a cab to her apartment, but today she thought she might walk a few blocks and let the streets clear up. It took her about an hour to reach the end of Belltown, and by then she was flushed in the face, having to dig around in her purse for a tissue. It was six o'clock and getting dark, and Wallingford was still too far to walk in heels. At Denny, she saw a cab and raised her hand. The yellow car pulled up a little before her and turned off its sign. A tall, old man on the street seemed to appear out of the dark and opened the rear door.

"Excuse me!" she yelled. "Hey!"

The old man turned around slowly, looking at the young blonde woman approach him.

"Yes?" he said.

"Hi, look I'm sorry," Summer breathed, "but is there any way we can share this cab? It's getting dark, and…"

"Say no more. It would be my pleasure."

"Oh, thank you!"

Inside, the driver asked where to take them to, and the old man motioned to Summer.

"Please, you first," he smiled.

"Oh, really? Well, thank you, um, Fourty-Fifth and Densmore, please." The cab took off and creaked left onto Broad Street in time for the light, running past the speed limit and blowing under the monorail. The driver slowed down, happy to take his time with two fares around Lake Union.

Summer looked at the old man from the sides of her eyes. He smelled odd, like maybe he was a butcher or worked with leather, but there was a slight essence of Brut, or some other cologne. She had the quick notion that he looked evil amid the séance of glowering green coming from the dashboard lights, almost as though he were not real but a mannequin bobbing up and down in the backseat of the cab as it drove the uneven roads. It was as though he was trapped still by some strange percussive gloom attempting to hold root deep in the wrinkles of his face, with the aim of warping whoever he was. He was a specter.

She tremored a little and looked at him full-on. Summer could make out a long nose over a deep sunken mouth below his wide hat. *I bet it's a Stetson*, she thought.

"How do you like Seattle?" the old man asked her. His voice was soft, about above a whisper.
"It's nice," Summer said, "I've lived here long enough to know I'll never get used to the winters, but the summers

more than make up for that." She blushed a bit, knowing she talked because she was nervous and wanted some sort of vocality present in the cab. The silence was too much for her, and the old man's smell had become intoxicating in the worst way. She wanted to lurch her lunch and then remembered what Jeremy talked about that afternoon; that poor kids' arm wrapped in tin foil.

"Are you alright?"

Summer held her breath before she answered, "Yes, excuse me, I just remembered something in today's paper."

"Oh? What was it?"

She cracked her window, "There was an arm found in Occidental Park. You know, down in Pioneer Square? God, I just think it's so awful. They say it was a kid's, too." The old man immersed himself more into the green dashlights, scooting up in his seat. He turned his head to the left and looked at Summer; she could make-out only half of his face now, and the old man's eye mawed at her, pure black.

"My, that is awful," he said, "Have they any leads to the culprit?"

"I haven't heard, but I sure hope so. That's just…it's just so—"

"Scary?" he interrupted.

Summer laughed, releasing her pent-up nerves, "Well, yeah." He leaned back and wiped his palm on his knee. Summer could hear the rasping of his skin over the brown fabric. The old man turned to her again, "I'm sure they will catch whoever is responsible. Sickness like that always takes its toll on the one it afflicts. Eventually."

"Yeah," Summer said.

The cab pulled up Stone Way and stopped at a red light. Drizzle began to fall, and the cabby took a right onto Forty-Fifth. "You can pull over up here," Summer said, and she began to peruse through her purse. The old man laid his hand on hers, "Oh no, I wouldn't think of it. Please, my treat." Summer gave a start at his hand. It was large and gloved, and she felt he withheld its weight from fully resting on hers. She focused on her red nails until the wipers of the cab became louder and she was overcome with an immense chill, like a strange, tiny hair had feathered the nape of her neck. "If you insist," she said, and forced a smile.

"Oh I do," the old man whispered, withdrawing his hand, "it's not everyday I garner the pleasure of sharing a cab with a beautiful young lady." Summer opened her door and stepped out. Feeling a strain of guilt she bent down and leaned back in, "Thank you. My name is Summer, I hope I didn't take you too far out of your way." The old man pushed his head a bit toward hers.

"Really, it's my pleasure, Summer. I am Lincoln Meab, and no, I only live a few minutes away," he withdrew, "have a good night."

"You too, and thank you again."

She shut the door and walked around the car to the sidewalk.

The cab passed her, and she looked to wave at the old man but saw he was absent from the backseat. She reeled around and saw a couple approaching her; behind them were the small houses leading down Forty-Fifth, and a few straggling people caught in the rain. She hurried across the street and went to the bricked nook where her apartment door beckoned safety. Summer was cool and precise, putting her key in the lock and shifting herself inside. She waited at the glass door, looking out.

A girl can never be too careful, she told herself.

The carpet in her complex was a gross pea color, and she figured it was well enough the main entry hall was just that: a hall. She checked her mail, struggling with the small key, and found nothing inside. The elevator was antiquated and she never liked riding it, but her feet were tender from walking all that way downtown.

She pressed the faded button, waiting for the dented doors to flush open. It took almost two minutes for it to come down two floors and reach her. She peered at the glass door looking out to the street one last time before getting in, not really minding the brown figure she partially saw bursting out of view on the sidewalk; not until the elevator doors closed around her did her heart began to jog.

On the way up, she refrained from thinking, afraid of anything possible or logical either way. She stood still and waited. The doors warbled and the wide hall presented itself. She felt calmer seeing her own door down to the right; there was no way that old man followed her, and even so, how could he get in, or know her unit number?

I told him my name…

She was scaring herself. She knew it. It was Jeremy's fault. Him and that horrible, disturbing story in the paper. When her apartment door was shut, locked, and double latched, Summer threw her purse on the couch and kicked off her heels, running her hand in her long wet hair. A glass of wine and a hot shower would do her good. It was only seven, and Wheel of Fortune was about to come on. She always wondered if Pat and that girl were married, or dating at least; maybe they were just having an affair.

Summer laughed a little out loud. "See?" she said, "You were just spooked by that stupid story. It's already forgotten. Harmless old man. He did pay my fare after all. And I did kinda steal his cab."

She poured a glass of cheap Pinot Grigio and went to her bedroom to change, seeing the copy of Smallcreep's Day on her stand; she felt she would have to return it to Jeremy unstarted. She undressed and headed to the bathroom, thinking and half talking to herself as most people living alone do. "It always takes so long to heat up, I better start the water."

She was feeling better and decided she would turn on the television with the volume up, so she could hear it in the shower.

Later, she sat on the couch in her favorite robe and picked at a few leftover bits of chicken and rice from her date with Johnny Terrance the other evening. The nightly news was on; she felt immediate dread, but turned up the volume, compelled nonetheless. The news anchor clipped his smile and became serious:

"...and in Pioneer Square last night, a gruesome sight was found by a Seattle city worker. Police are still investigationg, and are asking anyone with any information to please contact them. We go live now to William Sero..."

Summer was overcome with the strong urge to brush her hair. William Sero appeared on the screen and rounded a bench in Occidental Park. She reached into her purse on the couch next to her, and was reminded very strongly of the old man; did she recall him dropping something in her purse?

William Sero spoke:
"Good evening, yes, police are still as yet unsure whether this recent discovery is at all linked with any of the missing women found in the outlying areas of Seattle, but are not ruling out the possibility that the Green River killings may be connected. At around nine o'clock last night a city

worker came to this park and discovered a severed arm wrapped in several layers of tin foil, left right here, on this bench. What is more disturbing is the fact that police now know it is part of a child's arm. When police arrived, they discovered an additional thirteen teeth in the area surrounding the bench. This has local forces very concerned..."

Summer grabbed her brush, but felt something else in the palm of her hand. As she pulled it out, she found an ear. It was so small, and looked folded in half with dark staples; at first, she was unable to process it for what it was. Her scream was low and guttural as she pushed everything in her hands away from her body, standing up. The little ear lay in front of the television, as if listening to the anchors talk mock concern over what was found in the park the night before.

* * * *

A call came in, and Michael Lyonson let it ring. The heater under his desk was on the fritz again, and the pack of Merits by his papers became appetizing for the third time that hour; he shook one out, picking up the phone. "Hello?"

A sardonic, tired voice, tinny on the line, informed him of a call made two hours ago. A woman named Summer Tanzy had phoned into the police station to report a suspicious man she believed was responsible for leaving that arm in Seattle.

Michael Lyonson wrote down Summer's name and, looking at the time of night, asked if she was planning on going into the station to make a statement. "*A unit was already sent to her apartment; they took her statement there.*"
"…mm," he exhaled blue smoke, "where's the unit now? On their way back? What's the car number?" He wrote that down.
"*Their beat should be done by two; that's in an hour.*"
"Alright…get a hold of their dispatch and have them come on in; we shouldn't be waiting on information like that. Is

Reynolds on duty there? Right, have Reynolds hold their paperwork 'til I show up, but make sure he keeps them at the station. Yeah. I know I'll need to…yeah. Right…bye."

He hung up the phone and leaned back in his chair. The drive would be quick at this hour, but his timing would be a little close. He observed his study and reminded himself that this line of work never allowed much rest. He sighed and grabbed his gun and keys.

Michael Lyonson was waiting in the conference room when Summer showed up late for work the next day. Her boss approached her in the hall and asked if she was alright. She was confused until a strange ignominy washed her pure and shaking, having remembered again last night's ordeal; he must know, oh god, are the police here? She was led to the conference room where Lyonson sat, smoking.

"Ah, Miss Summer Tanzy?" he stood up and took her lame hand. "I'm Detective Lyonson, you can call me Mike if you like." He flashed a smile, "This should only take a few minutes. Please, have a seat."

"Oh, thank you," she said, almost dazed.

"I hear you had quite the night last night."

"Yes."

"Did you get any sleep?"

"…no, not really."

"Well, me neither, if that helps."

He offered her a cigarette, which she declined with a smile of her own. His pager went off and he clasped a big, muting hand to it. "Soon, no one'll have peace," he said, "once people know you're at their beck and call anywhere you go…boy, they just don't let up."

Summer laughed; she liked him.

She told him about the ear and the old man, and how she thought she saw him outside her apartment door after their cab ride together.

"The officers that came to your apartment last night told me you said his name was," he feigned thought, "…oh let me see here…Lincoln Meab, correct?"

"Yes."

"Alright…okay…"

"Did it belong to him?" Summer asked, low.

"What?"

"The ear, did it belong to that kid?"

"Afraid we don't know that just yet. It's possible, but…it's too early to tell." His pager beeped again.

"Why would he do it?" she asked, sheepish still.

"…Mm," Detective Lyonson became serious, and Summer was unsure how to read the look on his face, "you mean killing? Or leaving the body parts in public?"

Summer seemed caught in her own question, "Both, I guess."

"I think maybe he wants to get caught, if I'm to be honest," he said, "as for killing, well, who knows? He may not even be the guy."

"Is he in custody?!"

The detective pushed out his cigarette in the ashtray. "We have him, don't worry, but we don't have any evidence against him just yet."

Summer was hesitant. "Well, haven't you searched his home?"

"Eh, the warrant's under process, but if you were to call him out in a lineup, it would expedite things. The truth is, that would really help us out."

"Well, okay, I can talk to my boss and come with you—"

"No…no, we can wait, we have him for another nineteen hours, and he hasn't called for a lawyer. Why don't you come on down after work, say six o'clock? I'll pay for your cab fare, or I can send a car for you."

"I think I'm done with cabs for a while."

He chuckled. "Understandable. I'll pick you up myself then. That okay? I'll come up and escort you."

Summer felt the weight she had been carrying since last night lift off her back, "Oh that would be great, thank you Detective."

"Mike, please."

She smiled, "Mike."

As he got up to leave, he peered at her with his head a little toward his shoulder, "Could you maybe not tell any of your friends about this just yet? Confidential, you know…all that stuff."

Summer nodded a bit vigorous, eager to please him for some reason, "I wouldn't think of it."

He grinned, "Good. Good."

The rest of her day gurgled by; not really quick or slow, but almost like she hovered there in the office, just tipping the ground with her chair, watching her Friday go. At lunch, Jeremy offered to pay if she came down to Capital Grill with him. She felt obliged and chose to top her worst week ever in this way, but Jeremy was nice. While they ate, he asked her what was going on, and she answered, feeling a bit cool and aware of his interest in her as now more than just sexual.

"Yeah, I just had a run-in with this guy last night."

"Wow," Jeremy spoke through his tender steak, "did anything happen?"

"No, I mean, I'm fine and all, he just kinda' creeped me out. I thought I saw him outside my apartment door."

"Oh! He got inside?!"

Summer waved her salad fork, "No, no, no, outside the main door. You know. Where the…entry hall is…on the street." Her beat got down.

Jeremy cut into his food again, "Man, that's pretty scary."

"Yeah, I called the cops and two showed up pretty quick. I told them what all happened, now they want me to come in and pick him out of a lineup. I guess they went to his house and," she stabbed her fork playful at the air, "nabbed 'im!" They both chuckled.

"Why didn't you go when that detective was at the office earlier?" Jeremy asked.

Summer thought about it, "Um…well, he said there was no rush, so, you know, just after work."

"That's still a little weird."

"Jeremy…" Summer rolled her blue eyes. *If I told him about the ear, he'd just say something stupid.*

At six o'clock, Summer sat alone at her desk. The walls of her cubicle rose around her like white plasticine monoliths. She sat up and looked at her office doors, snorting and shaking her head. *What am I expecting? On the dot?*

Jeremy had been the last to leave. He was sweet for staying with her until they closed up the office, but she told him she would be fine when he asked to give her a lift, or if she needed to talk to someone. Maybe she would call Johnny after she got home from the station. When six fifteen rolled around, Summer was annoyed that she thought back on Jeremy, when he said during lunch that the detective asking her to come to the station later instead of sooner was odd. *What does he know?*

Six forty came and she was concerned enough to pick up the phone. She dialed the police station.

It rang for a while before a loud man answered. Summer asked for Detective Lyonson. The man on the other line rumbled, "Who now?"

"Detective Lyonson, please. I'd like to talk to Detective Lyonson."

"Ma'am, you got the right department?"

Summer panicked, "Well…I don't know…he didn't give me a card," when she began to describe the detective she found she had been placed on hold. She hung up the phone and decided not to call again.

That was weird, she thought, and simply stayed in her chair for lack of knowing what to do.

It was five minutes past seven when she heard the office doors swing open.

"Hello?" she said, and jumped up to see who came in.

"I'm so sorry, Summer," Detective Lyonson approached her, his hands fanned out in apology, "today has been just hell, and when I found out what time it was—"

The breath came out of her, "Oh thank god," she laughed, "I was beginning to worry. I even called the station."

He took pause from her, walking slower, "You did?"

She was grabbing her things, talking in the ebb of her sudden elation, "Yeah, I was so confused because they seemed confused when I asked for you. I'm sure I just wasn't heard right. There was a lot of noise at the station, and then he asked if maybe I had the right department, and then…"

Detective Lyonson nodded his head and smiled real big, "Yep! I'm from the Tacoma department. I told these idiots up here to pay attention to any calls I might get from the bigwigs down the sound, but…they think they got things the way they like 'em, I guess."

Summer turned from looking at her desk and smiled at him. "Okay, I just need to lock up real quick," she said.

They rode in his car, a basic brown Ford. She attempted to start a conversation twice, but each time he just answered her queries with a nod or a "yeah." The radio was on, and the detective turned down on the volume knob:

"…*other news, two Seattle police officers were found shot this morning near*—" he switched it off and laughed, "Boy, that was some timing."

"What was that?" Summer asked.

Detective Lyonson ignored her and turned down onto First, "So, have you eaten anything?"

Summer had that vague, uneasy feeling that waits, holding its breath until its sure. "Not since lunch."

He lit a cigarette and let the smoke fill the car. She looked at him, wondering why he kept the window up, why he suddenly had an air of rudeness about him.

"What'd you have?"

The feeling sunk deeper into her stomach. "A salad."

The inside of his car struck her then as strange, out of place. *Aren't police supposed to have big police radios or something?*

"Have you taken a shit?"

Summer turned to him. "Excuse me?"

"I said, did you take a shit earlier?"

"I...I don't..."

"I just don't want you to make a mess when I kill you. I hate when people shit their pants."

Her throat became so tight her first thought was *don't choke.*

"...are you a detective?"

He laughed out loud, and she reached for the door handle, wanting to flee the vulgar braying of his laughter more than anything. The door was locked and she saw too late his immense elbow coming at her face. She dragged herself off the window and felt the car come to a stop. Michael Lyonson began to beat her with both fists unabated.

*   *   *   *

"…and tell Reynolds good job. Yes. Yeah, I got her. Yeah, we're at Meab's now. No, I took care of that earlier, that's why…yeah. Well, he has the vats. Look, I couldn't just come over here with the girl in tow, right? He's never seen me before. Right…yeah. She called the station…no, it doesn't matter. Have you seen that monster he has down there? Look, I don't know, I'm sure we'll get Irion's…yeah, and then we'll know where to…yeah…"

Summer came to, groggy. She adjusted her eyes and peered around, feeling pain. She could barely see, but everything her eyes did catch shone like meteor-light, shooting and blurring the objects she knew as a table and a wall, but cast in far more frightening versions of themselves. She had difficulty breathing through her nose, and when she moved to touch it, she found her hands were bound behind her.

I must be in a chair, her inner voice drawled like a whining toddler. *Oh God, where am I?*

"…hey, like I said, I'm not sure either. We'll be contacted. No. C'mon, that only happens if you stop doing what he tells you, like Meab…"

Summer could hear Detective Lyonson talking to someone, and figured he was on the phone.

"Yeah…yeah, I dumped him in one of his lye pits he keeps down…yeah…they're pretty deep…no, I can't say…look, I really…I can't…yeah, I'm saying I don't know. I mean, he disposes of the no-good parts in the pits…yeah, I think he got tired. Yeah, tried to get caught. Have you seen this thing down here? Hey wait a sec, hold on…"

She realized she was making a noise from her throat, and the detective had stopped talking. She felt, more than heard, the approaching footfalls of Lyonson coming to get her, and she whimpered.

She struggled at first, but gave up when he hit her. Summer was being moved, and could tell it was darker where she went; that this area she passed through somehow felt closer. Summer guessed that he dragged her by the back of her chair into a hallway. She heard a door creak open, and a smell that both sharpened and sickened her bruised senses willowed around her.

"Jesus Christ," she heard Lyonson cry out. "Jesus, this is some shit, though."

Her chair crashed over each step leading down into Lincoln Meab's basement; every consecutive thump scaring her more and more. Even beyond this, she was aware of the smell; how it excited and shamed and constricted her.

Lyonson left her and plowed up the stairs, closing the door. Alone now, Summer could hear low running power; a hum in the corner somewhere. Her eyes adjusted in the dark room, but she was, in a way, relieved to be here. Not having to squint her blustered face against those brighter mimics of furniture upstairs gave her a slight sinew of reprieve; then her situation resurfaced, and drowned her in real despair. And then there was that smell, putrid and like a foreign garnishment adorning the stale sweat of the cold mortared walls.

The red blur in the corner she came to recognize as a small heater; one of the open coiled ones her mother always told her to be careful around. At the wall to her left were two mounds covered by flat steel doors hinged to the floor; puddles lay around them. Her head hazed up to the ceiling. It was high for a basement, and she had the queer memory that houses here were usually built without basements. Then, following along the ceiling, she saw it, the morass of flesh and limbs as big as a car, swelling like a whale in the dank back-end across from her; dead arms and feet curled up, withered and blackened around the steadying steel wires bolted into the raftered ceiling like nightmared vines. The thing vesiculated over the harsh wires rooted through portions of its rotting mass. She was completely without thought, staring at this.

It was only when one of the heads lolled amid the others, pushing them aside and limping beneath a slanted eave of legs draped with stapled elbows made to point at the sky that she pissed herself. When the small head hung out further and tilted back, showing its tiny white face, she screamed. The child's mouth opened too, struggling against the laces that halfway clamped it shut.

Michael Lyonson came roaring down the stairs, "Yelling won't do you any good Summer! This place is…" He saw what she looked at, blubbering in her chair.

"Yeah, that thing," he said, "Meab's job." Lyonson began to talk to himself, "Yeah, shit, I gotta take care of that, too." Summer croaked, and attempted to find the voice she just used, "…it moved…"

Lyonson pulled off a big hack knife from Meab's surgical bench, "What's that?"

"…moving…"

"This psycho-meat over here? It's just dead parts! Shipped from…" He flared his nostrils and let the knife hang in his hand. "Look! It ain't gonna get you, I am! I'm gonna flash your neck wide open!" And as he moved toward her, they both heard the twang of taut wires pulled past their load. Lyonson turned around and jumped, dropping the knife.

Summer looked at the big man above her; how he crouched down and plucked the heavy blade from the floor.

"Jesus," he smiled, "that scare you too?"

Summer's mouth quirked some; she was unable to see around Lyonson.

Did it…

"Thought that damned thing up and moved," he said.

Did it really move?

Shrugging it off, Lyonson stared at Summer, then grabbed her head, ensnaring her blonde hair in his fingers. "I'll say this," he said, "you sure are pretty. But I gotta slice ya; you know I do. I just gotta—"

Another sound suspended their moment together, and Lyonson turned his face again to peer at the warped limbs on the wires, thinking it resembled a large, over-done spider more than anything; *or really, one of those Hindu gods*, he thought, *with all those arms and legs flailing around.*

"The hell is going on?"

He walked away from her with the knife at his side. "You see that?" he said "Thing's movin'…"

Summer watched Lyonson get near the vibratory giant, and wondered if she really did see that tiny white face earlier. Had it moaned something? Lyonson peeked behind the show of Meab's work, positioning his face among the treated body parts like he was nosing through a group of branches, trying to tell what hid beyond the foliage.

"…no shit…I.V.'s…was Lincoln feeding this thing!?"

It lurched like it begged attention, resounding and shaking the rafters, spreading dust in the air. Lyonson scattered back, tripping on several of the legs curled up like J's, knocking them broken on the floor. The sudden release of leverage dropped the totem enough to snap two or three wires from the ceiling, collapsing the monster to one side. Summer saw the white face again; how it bobbed with the other heads along the chest piece made of little crossed arms. She saw its tiny black-hole-of-a-mouth part in shock and confusion, its green eyes wide open on her. As it hung, she was unable to refute a noticeable scar in the segment there; a piece missing, as if it were placed there and then taken off with intent. *Was that the arm in the park?* she thought. *Is that where it went?* She wanted to scream until she drowned in her noise, but it collapsed before she tried. Summer saw a pressing-out where looser joints were sewn, as though something small fought from inside; soon a weak wheeze came from the creature, and all motion ceased. She could hear the muffled yells of Lyonson beneath it, until that ceased as well.

The heater clicked, and Summer could find no other focal point to change her gaze from the curling left hand of Lyonson sticking out from beyond the chaotic curdle of limbs, his own arm appearing as just one more among the others, albeit larger and fresher. Some of the heads had rolled off, resting in separate areas. Summer, however quickly, believed they felt relieved to have personal space again. Her hands were hurting in hot waves; she needed to get blood to them. At last, she sent her eyes searching for the knife Lyonson grabbed. She had to get out; she had to call for help. *But how?*

She saw it in movies all the time, people roped-up in chairs; she had to kick off her heels.

I need to be on my side…

Summer was afraid to get hurt again. The floor was hard, and her head was killing her. Maybe if she scooted up and used the faggot of kids as a buffer—but she was getting ahead of herself. *Where was the knife? Was Lyonson right handed?* The knife was a big one, it had to be here. Then she had the shocking thought: *unless it's stuck between him and…that.*

She heard something, and let it engulf her panicking heart: a low beeping, Lyonson's pager going off, the sounds muffled. Summer remembered this morning when Lyonson put his hand to it in the conference room. He was left handed, and she felt a small victory at this, looking over at the latched mounds by the wall. The knife lay there in a cloudy puddle. Her mind made up, Summer wobbled to the patchwork of decimated bodies. There was no blood where the limbs had broken, and this gave her a weird image of cockroaches. She thudded on top of it. It was hard, and something snapped beneath her. *Oh god*, she dry heaved over a portion of fingers made to look like a small coach wheel, and being this close, inches away from the surface, she saw teeth everywhere. The whole of it was covered in little baby teeth, some inserted so the sharp roots stuck out. They pricked her shoulder, and that sensation urged more panic and more fear until she was sure she would go insane. Summer collapsed off of it, not caring about hurting herself anymore. Her face landed close to what remained of the heads. It took her some time to realize she was staring into that child's green eyes, the one that moved; the one that opened its mouth and tried to sound out something so frightening that Summer had pissed. Its nose was gone, and in its place were two rows of teeth.

She rushed away from it, writhing backward to the mounds and the knife. *Okay*, she thought, *I'm here, I'm here.* The water, or whatever it was, smelled foul, and she took to holding her breath when she could. The liquid was beginning to itch. Summer finessed her soaked feet out of her heels and stretched her toes through the web of pantyhose, pushing on any leverage she might find in the floor there. She was able to maneuver up a little, flaying her bound hands in the hopes of finding the knife. Cursing, she pushed herself further into the puddle, swiping her hands on the edge of the surgical saw. The pain made her squeal. She touched it again, cutting herself more. The water was beginning to burn, and she smelled a gross vapor coming off of her. Frantic, Summer forwent any subtlety and used a crazed energy to careen her knees against the floor, lifting herself just enough to land her hands on the wide knife. Some of the liquid splashed her face. Her fingers typed the blunt end of the blade, feeling where to grab. She found the handle and throttled it, shuffling her body along the floor, out of the puddle and back to dry land.

It took her a long time, but she cut the rope at her wrists. One thing they never showed in the movies, Summer told herself, was the part where the victim has to wait for feeling to come back into their limbs, like she had to before she could free her ankles from the chair. In that time, waiting, not sure how to move or turn, she almost fell asleep, and she might have, had Lyonson's pager not beeped again. Her body still burned, and her breath labored as half-muddled ideas formed inside her rattled brain. Ideas about home and work—*Johnny, what do I look like?*

Summer needed to see herself, she had to wash herself, she had to save herself, and where was her purse? *What time is it? Why me!?*

But soon came the thought of water—real, cooling, healthy water—trickling away any other concern.

She pulled her hands to her face and flexed her fingers; there was blood, sticky and scarlet along her arms. The cuts were deep where she swiped the knife, and the burning of new circulation mixing amidst caustic liquid sent her into a panicky spin of action. One moment, Summer lay on the floor; another, she was stamping up wooden steps into the house. She found herself standing by a door with curling carpet at her dirty feet. She wavered side to side. The hallway smelled empty, and the house was quiet; vacancy permeated every cranny, a vacuous guest long ingested into the home, now living like an imbibing cancer, consuming all noise and motion of life and joy. When she was young, she had this same feeling when left to stay with her grandmother; that silent, self-diluting possession of bored adventure among old, white-halled bookshelves and larger-than-life A/C filter vents that she sometimes unscrewed in hopes of finding some magical world she could crawl into. But in the end, it was always dark there, just like it was here. Summer was losing a lot of blood, and being drowsy, opened the door in front of her. The grim kitchen light down the hall at her back went no further, and she stepped into the dawn-graying room.

Summer casually knew she was in a child's bedroom, not really caring, just looking; doing something while she waited. She felt frail. Small dolls and small things lined up neat and cared for along the bed's seafoam-green headboard. Summer, absent, frolicked her lewd fingers less on herself, and more on the teddy bears and Red Annie Ragdolls. She looked at the smiling girl with no legs in the pictures by the window. *I think I know her. I know that face…pretty green eyes.*

And she smiled back while letters of doodled thanks to Dr. Irion peeled at the walls. Sitting on the end of the bed, immersed in its damp feel, and not thinking what era the musty sheets belonged to, she played with her hair, catching the child's makeup mirror across from her. It was small too, like the dresser it backed; shattered at a bottom corner. Summer dismissed the battered woman sitting in front of her: it was another girl, not herself. Had she seen her around work before? She looked different. Summer focused on all the faceted girl-faced-images, and giggled at the strangeness; *there's so many...hers. I wonder how many?*

And Summer began to count the shes in the mirror, unable to hear the front door as it swung open with a concerned question. "Mike, you're pager dead!?"

Whitewash

By Nathan Hodgdon

This is a transcript taken from a video which appeared on every international media share website and network in the developed world. After the first day on the public video server Youtube, it received over 2.7 billion views and 958 million likes. On the second day, the video was removed from Youtube, and the file could not be found on any known server in the world. The following transcript is classified Top Secret.

Principal Subject: Day One, reporting in for the first time.

I'll begin this account with a brief summary of my investigation thus far. My name is David Faulkner, and I'm an independent investigative journalist. For years, I have heard rumors of a secret government cartel smuggling some sort of contraband right under the noses of the public. My first assumption was illegal narcotics, some CIA black ops, but as my investigation deepened, it gave credence to my gut feeling that it was something more. Several leads brought me to dead-ends; shifting delivery schedules, logistical variations, virtually nameless personnel. It would seem as if I had been chasing ghosts.

Until last week. A new source provided coordinates in the American Southwest where I could infiltrate the smuggling ring and provide a first-hand account of whatever illegal black ops were being perpetrated on American soil.

I am recording this on my iPhone en route to my destination with the intention of releasing it in a global podcast at the end of my investigation, assuming I am not discovered. If I am, I will upload what I can to my private server, and it will be safe to assume me dead.

My anonymous source has instructed me to speak to no one until I arrive. I have to sign off for now and hide my phone from nothing but the most invasive body cavity search.

Stop.

Principal Subject: Day Two, reporting.

Nothing to report yet, aside from infrequent garbage trucks and the like. The ruse is tense and I'm under constant—someone's coming.

Stop.

Principal Subject: Day Four, reporting.

Due to the close call on Day Two, I decided to postpone an entry until I could ensure total privacy. The bathroom stall was too conspicuous, though if I am caught in this nearby field after dark, it'll still be way beyond explanation, but I'm willing to risk it in the event they figure out who I am; I must transmit my recordings before they make me disappear.

Sometime after noon on Day One, I arrived on foot at a dilapidated stretch of structures along an abandoned highway. I walked past a gas station with an old mechanic's shop behind it, followed by a greasy diner with a burned out neon sign, until I discovered a ramshackle farmhouse and barn situated a ways off the road, which I soon learned is where the crew sleeps.

I approached the gas station with confidence, my bluff long prepared and held steady in my mind. An old timer sporting a salt and pepper mustache sat on one of the four old-fashioned gas pumps. He studied me intently, his body language casual and relaxed. As I was about to speak, I felt as though I crossed a threshold into another world; my bluff, my name, the words on the tip of my tongue; all were snatched from my thoughts.

"You got a stutter?" the old man asked me, staring through bushy eyebrows. I fought to regain my poise, even if I felt like I had just thrown back several shots of tequila.

Since I couldn't remember my name—my real one or my fake one—I went with the first thing that came to mind. I was looking for work; that's what my source said to tell anyone if asked. The old timer just sits there and stares at me. My stomach churns, and I'm fearing I blew my cover, but I manage to keep my jaw steady, neither smiling nor flinching. Apparently satisfied, the old timer tells me to go on inside the gas station, and I'll find what I need.

Others came along after I did. I later saw another straggler who had a story to tell, and the old timer directed him to the service shop. I haven't seen him since that first day; my memory is pretty fuzzy most times. But I do know most folks who go into the service shop don't come out.

That first day, not much happened. I wandered around the gas station doing menial tasks on a hastily scrawled list. The old timer had me fill a few gas tanks, but only for certain cars. A few folks rolled through here only to hear our pumps were empty or broken. I'm still not sure what system they use to determine who gets gas, but it's obvious to see that John Q. Public is refused service.

Day Two was even weirder. Several large garbage trucks and dump trucks drove through here. All of us workers are expected to be nearby whenever any kind of trucks roll through, though most of us don't do much except watch the others work. It's also weird that no names are used. We just look, nod, point; whatever.

I noticed times where the waitress at the diner would come out, offering lemonade to all the gas station work crew, which was about ten of us besides the old man. While this occurred, the truck driver would get out and goes inside the diner. What's weird is I remember seeing the truck drive off, but without anybody in the driver's seat. I began memorizing the driver's faces on Day Three, and it's like the same guy goes in and out of the diner all day long. There's definitely something going on with that.

As for today's official entry, Day Four was completely dull. No trucks, and only two civilian vehicles. The only thing out of the ordinary was the old timer suggesting I get a bite to eat at the diner instead of grabbing a hoagie from the gas station. For some reason, I had a craving for a chocolate shake, even though I'm allergic to chocolate. I didn't have any money; oh yeah, I lost my wallet yesterday. Not sure what happened to it, but at least I had my fake ID and all. I told the waitress I didn't have any cash, but she said my bill could go on the gas station's tab. Instead of the shake, I order some coffee and a sandwich. I can tell it pissed her off, 'cause the coffee was cold and the sandwich was staler than a hunk of cardboard. Why was I telling that again? Oh yeah, it was the first time I went in there. I can see why business ain't booming. We'll see what happens tomorrow. Hopefully, I'll find some kind of evidence soon.

Stop.

Principal Subject: Day Six. Heh.

By today, I feel like I've been here forever; recalling my old life as an investigative journalist is almost a dream.

sob

I can't even remember my mom's face. What is it about this place?

Nothing more to report. If I can't get any deeper, then I'm outta' here.

Stop.

Principal Subject: Day Seven.

I'm sick of it. I spaced out for half an hour today; at least thirty minutes just staring out at the horizon. I don't know what's going on with me, but tonight, I'm making a break for it.

Stop.

Principal Subject: Day Fourteen, from what I can figure.

I intended to get out while the gettin' was good on the night of Day Seven, but I was so worn out that I fell into my bunk in the farmhouse, and didn't wake up 'til next morning. This kept happening for several nights, with each day bringing more and more memory loss. All the days are still blurred together in my mind, and I can only keep track of certain times I crashed at night.

A few days ago, on Day Twelve, I think, I went over to the diner again, just as I had daily since the boss' suggestion. That day, I gave in to my hankerin' and had a chocolate shake. Maybe it's 'cause the mysterious driver was in there, but I figured I might as well give it a shot.

Naturally, I was puking everywhere a few minutes later, but the waitress and driver didn't seem to care. They were too busy staring out the window, and that's when I saw it. The walls of the garbage truck collapsed to either side, revealing a bunch of metal drums with a symbol I couldn't recognize.

As if on cue (it probably was), this black helicopter comes out of nowhere, but I can tell nobody else sees it. Saw it. Nobody saw it, because they didn't take their eyes off the metal drums.

The jet black helicopter had glowing red instrument panels, visible even in the bright of day. Additionally, there was a gossamer, bluish bubble around it that pulsed outward in regular cadence. After several brief flashes, the bubble remained constant, and only then did the driver get out of the vehicle.

A second person revealed himself, identical to the driver, having sat in the midst of the metal drums. He pulled a lever, which moved the flatbed up and over, sliding the drums onto an arranged metal pallet. The driver then seated himself into his truck and drove away, as if nothing had happened; as if there wasn't a frickin' helicopter emitting a blue light in the middle of the air.

I didn't get to see what happened afterward because the waitress whirled around and saw me looking. She pretended it was nothing, and had me get a mop to clean up my mess. I heard her call someone, who turned out to be the boss at the gas station. From that moment on, I worked at the diner, mopping the floor and doing dishes. Every day, several trucks came, except for today, which gave me the time to make my entry; something I have wanted to do for the past several days.

I've managed to get a glimpse of what happens after the drivers leave. It seems like their twin sits among the barrels on the metal pallets, waiting for a laser scan from the black helicopter. During these deliveries, the guys I worked with among the gas station crew stand around like statues, though an occasional one will wander around like a mental patient. If one gets too close, the skinny little twin to the truck driver makes a whipping motion at him, forcing him back. At first, I thought he actually hit whoever got too close with a whip, but I watched him do it one time when the driver left the diner, and it seems like the glass on the doors and windows of the diner polarize the light to make it visible, because with the door open, I saw nothing but an empty hand.

After the helicopter scans the drums, it drops a tow line and hauls the metal pallet up into it. I didn't realize how much weight a helicopter could hold, but then this helicopter looks quite odd. Sometimes the midget comes into the diner, other times he goes into the gas station and talks to the old man.

One thing I have noticed; ever since I started working in the diner, my memory has improved greatly. I watched the gas station work crew; they look like insects to me, mindlessly droning about. I wonder if I would've looked the same to a casual observer? I'm sure it has something to do with that black helicopter; exposure to its blue light or something. Since this diner seems to be shielded somehow, I hope to make more progress on figuring out their operation.

And to whoever may be listening, know that I managed to get photographs. I won't be able to include them in this video without some editing software, but I'll try to upload them somehow. My shift is nearly up, and they'll expect me for bed soon, so I better go. Until next time.

Stop.

Principal Subject: Day Seventeen, reporting.

I've gotten my bearings back, so much as I can figure. I've been able to make records on my iPhone, though I haven't been unable to determine exactly what the cargo actually is.

Nor have I been able to get any sort of information on anyone here at the facilities. Conversation is pretty much non-existent; an easy stipulation to keep when my mind was somehow dulled, but now that I can link coherent thoughts together, not talking to anyone has been difficult.

I haven't seen the old timer in days, save for a few glances through the windows of the diner. Despite all of this intel, I feel no closer to cracking the case. Maybe I need to be bolder and trail the old man.

Stop.

Principal Subject: Day Nineteen, reporting.

I'm at an impasse right now. Do I upload my video journal and possibly give myself away, or do I hang tight and hope I didn't blow my cover?

See, today I got ballsy and dumped out some cleaning materials so I'd have an excuse to mosey back over to the gas station. After the helicopter left for the first time today, I went over to the gas station to retrieve the supplies, as well as rub shoulders with the old man. I had to wait a minute for him to come inside, which raises the question of where he is whenever the helicopter is there.

When he finally walked in, I asked as nonchalantly as I could who the midget was. The old man glared at me with eyes so hot I almost melted. He told me it didn't matter, and then stormed off to his usual perch on one of the gas pumps. My gut tells me trouble is on the way.

Stop.

Principal Subject: Day Twenty-Four

I'm sick. It's freezing down here. There's no heat and no light. I'm only keeping track of the days by how much I sleep, and that's just a guess. I haven't eaten since Day Nineteen. At first, I thought they discovered me, but they haven't found my iPhone, so I think I just pissed off the old man. Oh well. I'm going to die at this rate, so I might as well make a final entry. I already tried to transmit, but I'm too far underground. I guess my journal dies with me.

I'd tell you about being grabbed from my bed, dragged through the mechanic's shop and hauled down a secret tunnel into a cell block, but you won't hear it. No one will, save for an interrogator who takes my phone away from me.

God Almighty, it wouldn't be hard to heat this place. It's not like I'm in a medieval dungeon; the walls are all some sort of composite plastic.

The door is opening. I. . . need to. . . stash this.

gasp

God Almighty, I'll never get used to that.

sob

Why did I ever agree to this. . ?

indistinct background noise

Who are you? What do you want with me?

indistinct background noise

Say something!

indistinct background noise

What's that door?! Where are you taking me?!

clanging noises

Oh my God…what are you?

The remainder of the transcript implies a conversation of alternate personalities through the single voice of the principal subject. The alternate personalities are designated Alpha and Omega.

Subject Alpha: Have a seat, Mr. Faulkner.

Principal Subject: *unintelligible*

Subject Alpha: Screaming will only tire your diaphragm and hinder attempts at communication.

Principal Subject: Get out of my head!

Subject Alpha: I assure you no entity resides in your head, other than your own brain.

Principal Subject: Leave. . . my. . . thoughts…alone!

Subject Alpha: That is a request I must decline.

Principal Subject: What do you want with me?

Subject Alpha: I shall determine what you are doing here, and how you evaded our security sweeps for so long. You can make this process easier by telling us whom you are working for.

Principal Subject: *laugh* I. . . am work. . . *grunt*…working for myself!

Subject Alpha: I doubt this very much, Mr. Faulkner. If you are not going to cooperate, we can excise the pertinent information from you postmortem as necessary.

Principal Subject: Kill me. Go ahead. Watch this... *gasp*

Subject Alpha: Mr. Faulkner, any attempts to end your life prematurely will—

Principal Subject: There! See this?! It's an iPhone, and it's got signal, you red-eyed bastard! Not you or your tinman thugs can stop me now. It's uploading journal entries from the duration of my stay here to my private server, as well as photographic evidence of your distribution operation. Kill me if you want, but the truth is about to be at the fingertips of anyone with an Internet connection.

Subject Alpha: You know nothing, Mr. Faulkner. You know not from where our shipments come, nor where they go. You know not even the contents, as your own journals attest.

Principal Subject: It's only a matter of time, you freak.

Subject Alpha: Indeed, it is so. We control the transfer of information on a quantum level. Should your data bypass our internal and external security measures, it will be, as you say, only a matter of time before our search algorithms locate any persons who extrapolate damaging information from your journal. They shall be found, and detained indefinitely. You have accomplished nothing, Mr. Faulkner.

Principal Subject: Then why do you drag this on? My iPhone is still broadcasting; I'm sure you could shut it off. Why let this continue?

Subject Alpha: As I said, Mr. Faulkner, we wish to determine how you got as far as you did. Rest assured, however; your life is forfeit beyond scope.

Principal Subject: That still doesn't explain why you're allowing the broadcast.

Subject Omega: It is because they cannot, in fact, block it.

Principal Subject: What the hell? Who is this?

Subject Omega: I'm sorry I couldn't protect you. You had too much exposure to the pulses and it interfered with the interphasic apparatus you carry on your person. It should be recharging through the signal on your phone.

Principal Subject: I—I don't understand.

Subject Omega: You are carrying a device that your host can neither see nor touch; it prevents significant influence from his means of control.

Subject Alpha: But not for long, Mr. Faulkner.

Subject Omega: Do not heed their words. What are they doing to you now?

Principal Subject: The red-eyed freak with the wires in his head is sending robots toward me.

Subject Omega: Can they reach you?

Principal Subject: It doesn't appear so.

Subject Omega: Good. The interphasic field is operational for now. Anything you touch should be rendered inert. Listen, walk toward the console above the organic's head. Try to punch through it, if possible.

Principal Subject: That's crazy; how could I do that?

Subject Alpha: You cannot, Mr. Faulkner. It is impossible.

Principal Subject: I'll give it a shot.

Subject Alpha: *Unintelligible glitching noises*

Principal Subject: Everything's going to hell around here. The robots fell over; the floor is shaking.

Subject Omega: Get out of there, Faulkner!

Principal Subject: Oh, God! To any who may be listening, I just found one of the metal drums. I have to know what's inside.

Subject Omega: Faulkner, no, don't—

Principal Subject: I am now opening the drum…

Subject Omega: Faulkner, it's too dangerous!

Principal Subject: What the…I can see…

unintelligible speech

background noise

white noise

End transmission.

There's plenty more Aberrant Literature for you to experience…
Visit our blog for new and exclusive stories and articles at www.AberrantLiterature.com, and be sure to check out past and future volumes of the Aberrant Literature Short Fiction Collection.

Stay in touch with Aberrant Literature via:

Facebook: Aberrant Literature

Twitter: @AberrantLit

If you liked this Aberrant Literature Short Fiction Collection, please post a review at Amazon, and let your friends know about us. All honest and unbiased reviews are appreciated.

Stay tuned for more collections to come!

Author Contact Info and Bio:

Jason Peters – Editor – JasonAberrant@yahoo.com

Jason Peters is a Screenwriter, Author, and Founder/Editor-In-Chief of Aberrant Literature. Residing in Los Angeles, his works include the horror/comedy/crime-thriller screenplay *Obsidian*, and the short story *A Trial By Any Other Name*. He is actively writing his first novel, to be released in 2016, in addition to personally curating and editing each volume of the *Aberrant Literature Short Fiction Collection*. Please contact via e-mail to discuss business opportunities, and follow on Twitter @AberrantLit.

Carl Reid – Author – carlreid00@hotmail.com

Carl Reid is a native of Washington, DC with a lifelong passion for storytelling, particularly in film. Now residing in Los Angeles and pursuing a screenwriting career, his first feature film will be shot in his hometown in the summer of 2016, with more projects soon to follow. Carl has a penchant for stories that bring other worlds to life through the eyes of everyday characters, citing writers like Tolkien, Dick, Bradbury, Alan Moore, Ed Brubaker, and Peter David as significant influences.

Mark Daponte – Author – Markosborne2000@yahoo.com

Mark Daponte is a copy/blog writer for an advertising company in New York City. He has sold two short stories and three screenplays, while also punching up others' screenplays—because they don't punch back. Additionally, he is a freelance comedic copy editor/writer for the lifestyle websites Brave New Hollywood, (http://bravenewhollywood.com/) and A Life Ahead (http://www.alifeahead.com/) When he isn't sinking down to a five year old's level to make his eight and five year old sons laugh, he can be found seeking signs of intelligent life and good bargains in his hometown of Brooklyn, NY.

Ashton Macaulay – Author –Ashton.Macaulay@yahoo.com

Ashton Macaulay recently vanquished the beast of higher education, receiving a legendary master's degree in experimental psychology for his trouble. When he is not slaying mythical beasts with his trusty feline companion Stormageddon, he enjoys listening to vinyl, free-range, organic, locally roasted, gluten free coffee and a good pug. Other accomplishments include: Creation of The Pattison Chronicle (the world's best fake news blog), publishing on ABCTales.com/MacAshton, and conducting experimental trials for the gaming industry.

Author Contact Info and Bio (cont.):

M.T. Roberts – Author – tmtrp@hotmail.com

M. T. Roberts is the author of *The Night City*. Originally from Mississippi, he has called Seattle home for the past several years, and currently resides near Lake Union with his girlfriend and poodle—the author's cat would like to be mentioned, but as he is not on the lease, certain landlords my find his mention an unwelcome surprise. Growing up, M. T. Roberts had an appetite for science fiction and classic literature. He is an expert at napping, but a novice at sleeping, and overall adept at sitting up. He has a steady day job with a local wine importer, and usually drinks beer when writing into the long, cold nights.

Nathan Hodgdon – Author - nathanhodgdon1@gmail.com

Nathan is a jack-of-all-trades with an eclectic background that has deeply influenced his writing. Drawing from his love of history, the sciences, and world cultures, his favorite genres are fantasy, science fiction, and supernatural thrillers. With several freelance writing projects to his credit, he is currently pursuing his love of storytelling through novel-length works. Whitewash is Nathan's first traditionally published short story. He is a father of three, and lives with his family in the Pacific Northwest.

Author Contact Info and Bio (cont.):

Jared Wojcik - Graphic Design - <u>Jared.wojcik@gmail.com</u>

      Jared is a freelance Graphic Designer based out of Los Angeles, CA. He designed and created the Aberrant Literature logo, in addition to numerous other logos and design elements for prominent businesses, including Fortune 1000 companies. Please contact via e-mail to discuss design-related business opportunities.